"You want m... the most natural thing in the world."

Matt continued smoothly, "It doesn't have to be complicated."

The amusement in his dark face was the last straw. Georgie turned on him like a small green-eyed cat, her eyes spitting sparks as she shouted, "You are actually daring to proposition me? In cold blood?"

"Oh, is that what the matter is? You wanted a bouquet of red roses and promises of undying love and forever? Sorry, but I don't believe in either...."

VIVA LA VIDA DE AMOR!

They speak the language of passion.

In Harlequin Presents® you'll find a
special kind of lover—full of Latin charm.
Whether he's relaxing in denims or dressed
for dinner, giving you diamonds or
simply sweet dreams, he's got spirit,
style and sex appeal!

Latin Lovers is the miniseries
from Harlequin Presents®
for anyone who enjoys hot romance!

Helen Brooks loves to write emotional stories
about powerful heroes being tamed by warm,
lively heroines. She's created a Latin Lover to die
for in *A Spanish Affair....* Turn the page to meet
Matt de Capistrano—a gorgeous tycoon
no woman could resist!

Helen Brooks

A SPANISH AFFAIR

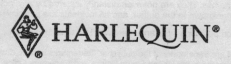

HARLEQUIN®

TORONTO • NEW YORK • LONDON
AMSTERDAM • PARIS • SYDNEY • HAMBURG
STOCKHOLM • ATHENS • TOKYO • MILAN • MADRID
PRAGUE • WARSAW • BUDAPEST • AUCKLAND

ISBN 0-373-12213-6

A SPANISH AFFAIR

First North American Publication 2001.

Copyright © 2001 by Helen Brooks.

Visit us at www.eHarlequin.com

Printed in U.S.A.

CHAPTER ONE

'THINGS are really that bad? But why on earth didn't you tell me?' Georgie's sea-green eyes were wide with shock as she stared into her brother's troubled face. 'I could have helped in some way.'

'How?' Robert Millett shook his blond head slowly. 'You couldn't have done anything, Georgie, no one could, and there was still an element of hope before that last contract was pulled out from under our feet. Old man Sanderson really ducked and dived for that one. But, as he's so fond of saying, all's fair in love and war.'

Georgie's smooth brow wrinkled in an angry frown. Mike Sanderson was a mean old man and she wouldn't trust him as far as she could throw him, and as she was a tiny, slender five foot four to Mike's burly six foot that wouldn't be far! 'He's an out-and-out crook,' she stated tightly. 'I just don't know how he can sleep at night with some of the tricks he pulls.'

'Georgie, Georgie, Georgie.' Robert pulled his sister into his arms and hugged her for a moment before pushing her away and looking down into her flushed face. 'We both know Mike's not to blame for the mess I'm in. I had to make some choices over the last months when Sandra was so ill, and even now I know I made the right ones. I don't regret a thing. If the business fails, it fails.'

'Oh, Robert.' This was so *unfair*. When Robert had discovered his beloved wife, Sandra, was suffering from a rare blood disorder that meant she only had a few months to live, he had devoted himself to making her last days happy ones, and taking care of their seven-year-old twins, David and Annie, and trying to shield them from as much pain as possible as their mother slowly faded away. Sandra and Robert had told no one the true state of affairs—not even Georgie had known Sandra's illness was terminal until four weeks before she had died.

That had been six months ago, and immediately she had understood what was happening. Georgie had packed her bags and left her wonderful, well-paid job in advertising and high-tailed it back to the family home to take some of Robert's burden in the last traumatic weeks of Sandra's illness.

She hadn't had to think twice about such a step—Robert and Sandra had opened their arms to her when, as a bewildered little girl of ten and newly orphaned, she had needed love and care. Now, thirteen years later, it was her turn to repay the tenderness and warmth they had lavished on her, which hadn't diminished a jot when their own children were born.

'What about the de Capistrano deal? They've already offered us the contract, haven't they? And the rewards would be brilliant.' Sandra had run the office side of Robert's building firm before she had become ill, and after a succession of temps had muddled through Georgie had had her work cut out the last few months to make sense of the paperwork. It didn't help that after the funeral Robert had retreated into a world of his own for some time, the strain of being Sandra's mainstay and support, as well as mother and father to the children, telling at last.

'De Capistrano?' Robert ran a tired hand through his thick hair, which immediately sprang back to its previous disorder.

Georgie noticed, with a little pang in her heart, that there were several strands of grey mixed with the honey-gold

these days. But then that wasn't surprising after all her big
brother had been through, she thought painfully. They were
all of them—David, Annie and herself—missing Sandra
like mad, but Sandra had been Robert's childhood sweet-
heart and her brother's grief was overwhelming.

'We'd need to take on more men and hire machinery to
make it viable, and the bank's screaming blue murder already. I had relied on the profit from this other job to finance de Capistrano's.'

'But we can go and see them and ask at least?' Georgie's
small chin stuck out aggressively, as though she was already doing battle with the pinstriped brigade. 'They aren't
stupid. They'll be able to see the potential, surely?'

'I'd have thought you were dead against the de
Capistrano deal after all your "green" rallies and such at
uni?' Robert remarked quietly. 'Animal rights, save the
hedgerows, Greenpeace… You were into them all, weren't
you?'

Georgie stared at him, her heavily lashed eyes narrowing.
Robert had been sixteen years of age when she was born,
their parents having long since given up hope of ever having another child. Consequently his attitude had always
been paternal, even before the car crash which had taken
their parents, and she had often rebelled against his staid
and—Georgie considered—prosaic views about a million
and one subjects dear to her heart. But now was not the
time to go into all that, she reminded herself, as she looked
into the blue of his worried eyes.

'That's a separate issue,' she said very definitely. 'If it's
a case of the de Capistrano contract or virtual bankruptcy
for you, I'll take the contract.'

'If they could hear you now…' Robert summoned up
something of a grin—his first one for days—which Georgie
took as a good sign.

'They can't.' It was succinct. 'So, how about approaching the bank?'

'Useless.' It was clear all Robert's normal get up and go had got up and gone. 'I've got de Capistrano himself coming in later this morning and he won't be interested in a building firm that's on the rocks.'

Georgie searched her mind frantically. 'Well, what about asking de Capistrano to finance the men and machinery on a short-term basis?' she suggested brightly. 'Once we got going we could pay him back fairly quickly, and it's common knowledge he is something of an entrepreneur and filthy rich into the bargain.'

'Exactly, and he hasn't got that way by doing anyone any favours,' Robert said cynically. 'His reputation is as formidable as the man himself, so I understand, and de Capistrano is only interested in a fast turnover with huge profits. Face it, Georgie, he can go elsewhere and have no hassle. End of story.'

Her brother stretched his long, lanky body wearily in the big leather chair behind the desk strewn with the morning's post, his blue eyes dropping to the fateful letter open in front of him. It stated that Sandersons—not Milletts—had been successful in securing the contract for the town's new leisure complex. A contract which would have provided the profit margin to finance the extra men's wages and hiring of the machinery for de Capistrano's job.

'But, Robert—'

'No buts.' Robert raised his head to take in his sister's aggressive stance. 'De Capistrano is a Sanderson type, Georgie. He knows all the right angles and the right people. Look at the deal we were going to discuss this morning; he negotiated that prime piece of land for a song some years ago and he's been holding on to it until the time was right to build housing. He'll get his outlay back a hundred times over on the sort of yuppie estate he is planning.'

'Yes, well...' Georgie wrinkled the small straight nose she'd inherited from her mother in disgust, unable to hide her real opinion any longer. 'I'm sorry, but I have to say destroying that beautiful land *is* out-and-out sacrilege! People have enjoyed that ground as a park in the summer ever since I can remember and the wildlife is tremendous. Do you recall that rare butterfly being found there the year I started uni?'

'Butterflies aren't good business.' Robert shrugged philosophically. 'Neither are wild flowers and the like, come to that, or putting family first and being less than ruthless. Maybe if I'd been a bit more like the de Capistranos of this world my kids wouldn't be in danger of losing the roof over their heads.'

'Don't say that,' said Georgie fiercely, her eyes sparking green flames. 'You're the best father and husband and brother in the world. You've already admitted you've no regrets in putting Sandra first and it was absolutely the right thing to do. You're ten times the man—a hundred times— de Capistrano will ever be and—'

'Have we met?'

Two blonde heads shot round as though connected by a single wire and a pair of horrified green eyes and amazed blue surveyed the tall dark man standing in the doorway of the small brick building that was Robert's office. The voice had been icy, and even if the slight accent hadn't informed Georgie this was de Capistrano she would have known anyway. The impeccable designer suit and silk shirt and tie sat on the tall lean body in a way that positively screamed unlimited wealth, and the beautiful svelte woman standing just behind the commanding figure was equally well

dressed. And equally annoyed if the look on the lovely face
was anything to go by. His secretary? Or maybe his wife?

And then Georgie's racing thoughts were focused on the
man alone as he said again, 'Have we met?' and this time
the voice had all the softness of a razor-sharp scalpel.

'Mr de Capistrano?' Georgie's normally clear voice was
more of a weak squeak, and as she cleared her throat nervously the black head nodded slowly, the deep, steel-grey
eyes piercingly intent on her face. 'I'm sorry... I didn't
know...' She took a hard pull of air before continuing more
coherently, 'No, Mr de Capistrano, we haven't met, and I
have no excuse for my rudeness.'

'So.' The furious anger in the frosty face hadn't diminished an iota.

'Mr de Capistrano.' Robert pulled himself together and
strode across the room, extending his hand as he said,
'Please understand. What you overheard was less a comment on you than an endeavour to hearten me. There was
nothing personal intended. I'm Robert Millett, by the way,
and this is my sister, Georgie.'

There was a pause which seemed to last for ever to
Georgie's tortured senses, and then the hand was accepted.
'Matt de Capistrano.' It was pithy. 'And my secretary,
Pepita Vilaseca.'

Georgie had followed her brother across to the others
and as the two men shook hands she proffered her own to
the immaculate figure at the side of the illustrious Mr de
Capistrano. This time the pause was even longer and the
lovely face was cold as the tall slim secretary extended a
languid hand to Georgie, extracting it almost immediately
with a haughty glance which said more clearly than any
words could that she had done Georgie the most enormous
favour. Pepita. Georgie looked into the beautifully made-

up ebony eyes that resembled polished onyx. Sounded like an indigestion remedy to her!

And then, as Robert moved to shake the secretary's hand, Georgie was forced to raise her eyes up to the dark gaze trained on her face, and acknowledge the reality of what she had imbibed seconds earlier. This was one amazingly…handsome? No, not handsome, her brain corrected in the next moment. Male. One amazingly *male* man. Overwhelmingly, aggressively male. The sort of man who exuded such a primal masculinity that the veneer of civilisation sat frighteningly lightly on his massive frame.

The leanly muscled body, the jet-black hair cropped uncompromisingly short, the hard good looks—

'Do you always…encourage your brother by doing a character assassination on complete strangers, Miss Millett?' Matt de Capistrano asked with arctic politeness, interrupting Georgie's line of thought and forcing her to realise she had been staring unashamedly.

She turned scarlet. Help, she breathed silently. Get me out of this, someone. He had held out his hand to her and as she made herself shake his, and felt her nervously cold fingers enclosed in his firm hard grip that sent frissons of warmth down to her toes in a most peculiar way, her mouth opened and shut like a goldfish in a bowl before she was able to say breathlessly, 'No, no, I don't. Of course I don't.'

'Then why today and why me?'

His voice was very deep and of an almost gravelly texture, the slight accent turning it into pure dynamite, Georgie thought inappropriately. 'I… You weren't supposed to hear that,' she said quickly, before she realised just how stupid that sounded.

'I'd worked that one out all on my own,' he said caustically.

Oh, how could she have been so unforgivably indiscreet?

Georgie's heart sank into her shoes. Her flat shoes. Which didn't help her confidence at all with this huge six-foot avenging angel towering over her measly five foot four inches—or perhaps angel was the wrong description. 'It was just an expression,' she said weakly. 'There was absolutely nothing personal in it, as Robert said.'

'That actually makes it worse, Miss Millett.' It was cutting. 'When—or should I say if?—anyone had the temerity to insult me I would expect it to be for a well-thought-out and valid reason.'

Well, hang on just a tick and I'm sure I can come up with several, Georgie thought darkly, forcing a respectful nod of her head as she said out loud, 'All I can do is to apologise again, Mr de Capistrano.' Which is exactly what you want, isn't it? Your full pound of flesh.

'You work here?'

Georgie thought frantically. If she said yes it might be the final death knell to any faint hope Robert had of persuading this man to finance the cost of the new machinery for a short time, but if she said no and the deal did go through he'd soon know she'd been economical with the truth!

'Temporarily,' she compromised hesitantly.

'Temporarily.' The lethal eyes demanded an explanation, but Robert—tired of being virtually ignored—cleared his throat at the side of them in a way that demanded attention. Matt de Capistrano paid him no attention at all. 'Does that mean you will be here for the foreseeable future, Miss Millett?'

Without your contract there isn't a future. It was that thought which enabled Georgie to draw herself up straight and say, as she met the icy grey gaze head-on, 'Not if you feel that would be inappropriate after what I've said, Mr de Capistrano.'

He blinked. Just once, but she saw she had surprised him. And then he swung round to face Robert, his dark aura releasing her as his piercing gaze left her hot face. 'I came here today to discuss a proposed business deal,' he said coldly, 'and I am a very busy man, Mr Millett. You have the financial details ready which my secretary asked you to prepare?'

Robert gulped. 'I do, Mr de Capistrano, but—'

'Then as we have already wasted several minutes of valuable time I suggest we get down to business,' Matt de Capistrano said tightly, cutting across Robert's stumbling voice.

What an arrogant, ignorant, overbearing, high and mighty—Georgie's furious adjectives came to a sudden halt as the grey eyes flicked her way again. 'I trust you have no objection to that, Miss Millett?' he asked softly, something in his face making it quite clear to Georgie he had known exactly what she was thinking. 'I take it you are your brother's...temporary secretary?'

Somehow, and she couldn't quite put a finger on it, but somehow he made it sound insulting. 'Yes, I am,' she responded tightly.

'How...convenient,' he drawled smoothly.

'Convenient?' It was wary.

'To have a ready-made job available like this rather than having to fight your way in the big bad world and prove yourself,' was the—to Georgie—shocking answer.

How dared he? How *dared* he make assumptions about her just because she had ruffled his wealthy, powerful feathers? That last remark was just plain nasty. Georgie reared up like a small tigress, all thoughts of appeasement flying out of the window as she bit out, 'I happen to be a very good secretary, Mr de Capistrano.' She had worked her socks off as a temp all through the university holidays in order to be less of a financial burden on Robert—one of her ten GCSEs being that of Typing and Computer Literacy before her A Levels in Business Studies, English and Art and Design—and every firm the temping agency had placed her with had wanted her back.

'Really?' Her obvious annoyance seemed to diminish his. 'You did a secretarial course at college?'

'Not exactly.' She glared at him angrily.

'My sister graduated from university two years ago with a First in Art and Design,' Robert cut in swiftly, sensing Georgie was ready to explode.

'Then why waste such admirable talents working for big brother?' He was speaking to her as though Robert and his secretary didn't exist, and apart from the content of his words hadn't acknowledged Robert had spoken. 'Lack of ambition? Contentment with the status quo? Laziness? What?'

Georgie couldn't believe her ears. 'Now look here, you—'

Robert cut in again, his face very straight now and his voice holding a harsh note as he said, 'Georgie left an excellent job a few months ago, Mr de Capistrano, in advertising—a job she was successful in obtaining over a host of other applicants, I might add. She did this purely for me and there is no question of it being a free ride here, if that is what you are suggesting. My wife used to run the office here but—'

'You don't have to explain to him.' Georgie was past caring about the contract or anything else she was so mad.

'But she died six months ago. Okay?' Robert finished more calmly.

There was a screaming silence for a full ten seconds and Georgie moved closer to Robert, putting her hand on his arm. She noticed the secretary had done the same thing to

Matt de Capistrano which seemed to suggest a certain closeness if nothing else.

'I'm not sure that an apology even begins to cover such insensitivity, Mr Millett, but I would be grateful if you would accept it,' the tall dark man in front of them said quietly. 'I had no idea of your circumstances, of course.'

'There was no reason why you should have.' Robert's voice was more resigned than anything now. He had the feeling Matt de Capistrano was itching to shake the dust of this particular building firm off his feet as quickly—and finally—as possible.

'Perhaps not, but I have inadvertently added to your pain at this difficult time and that is unforgivable.' The accent made the words almost quaint, but in view of the situation—and not least the big lean figure speaking them—there was nothing cosy about the scenario being played out in the small office.

'Forget it.' Robert waved a dismissive hand. 'But it is the case that I find myself in somewhat changed circumstances. We discovered this morning we had lost some vital work, work which I had assumed would finance the extra men and hire of machinery I need for your job, Mr de Capistrano.'

'Are you saying the estimate you supplied is no longer viable?' The deep voice was now utterly businesslike, and Georgie—standing to one side of the two men—suddenly felt invisible. It was not a pleasant feeling.

'Not exactly,' Robert replied cautiously. 'I can still do the job at the price I put forward, if my bank is prepared to finance the machinery and so on, but—'

'They won't,' Matt de Capistrano finished for him coolly. 'Are you telling me your business is in financial difficulties, Mr Millett?'

'I'm virtually bankrupt.'

Georgie couldn't stop the gasp of shock at hearing it put so baldly, and as the men's heads turned her way she said quickly, without thinking about it, 'Because he dedicated himself to his wife when she and the children needed him, Mr de Capistrano, *not* because he isn't a good builder. He's a great builder, the best you could get, and he never cuts corners like some I could mention. You can look at any of the work he's done in the past and—'

'Georgie, please.' Robert was scarlet with embarrassment. 'This is between me and Mr de Capistrano.'

'But you *are* a fine builder,' Georgie returned desperately. 'You know you are but you won't say so—'

'*Georgie.*' Robert's voice was not loud but the quality of his tone told her she had gone as far as she could go.

'I think it might be better if you waited in your office, Miss Millett,' Matt de Capistrano suggested smoothly, nodding his head at the door through which her small cubbyhole of a place was situated.

Georgie longed to defy him—she had never longed for anything so much in all her life—but something in Robert's eyes forced her to comply without another word.

For the first time since childhood she found herself biting her nails as she sat at her desk piled high with paperwork, the interconnecting door to Robert's office now firmly shut. She could just hear the low murmur of voices from within, but the actual conversation was indistinguishable, and as time slipped by her apprehension grew.

How long did it take to rip up a contract and say byebye? she thought painfully. Matt de Capistrano wasn't going to twist the knife in some way to pay her back for her rudeness, was he? Those few minutes in there had made it plain he'd never been spoken to like that before in his life, and a man like him didn't take such an insult lying down. Not that she had actually *spoken* to him when she'd insulted him, just about him. She groaned softly. Her and her big mouth. Oh, why, *why* had he had to come in at that precise moment and why had she left the door to her office open so he'd heard every word? And Robert. Why hadn't he *told* her how bad things were?

The abrupt opening of the door caught her by surprise and she raised anxious green eyes to see Matt de Capistrano looking straight at her, a hard, speculative gleam in the dark grey eyes. 'Daydreaming, Miss Millett?'

The tone of his voice could have indicated he was being friendly, lightly amusing in a pleasant teasing fashion, but Georgie was looking into his face—unlike the two behind him—and she knew different. 'Of course. What else do temporary secretaries do?' she answered sweetly, her green eyes narrowing as she stared her dislike.

He smiled, moving to stand by her desk as he said, 'I intend to phone your brother tonight from Scotland after certain enquiries have been made. The call will be of vital importance so can you make sure the line is free?'

'Certainly.' She knew exactly what he was implying and now added, 'I'll let all my friends and my hairdresser and beautician know not to call me then, shall I?' in helpful, dulcet tones.

His mouth tightened; it clearly wasn't often he was answered in like vein. 'Just so.' The harsh face could have been set in stone. 'I shall be working to a tight schedule so time is of the essence.'

'Absolutely, Mr de Capistrano.'

The grey gaze held her one more moment and then he swept past her, the secretary and Robert at his heels, and as the door closed behind them Georgie sank back in her seat and let out a big whoosh of a sigh. Horrible man! Horrible, horrible man! She ignored the faint odour of expensive aftershave and the way it was making her senses quiver and concentrated her mind on loathing him instead.

She could hear the sound of voices outside the building and surmised they must all be standing in the little yard, and, after rising from her chair, she peeped cautiously through the blind at the window.

Matt de Capistrano and his secretary were just getting into a chauffeur-driven silver Mercedes, and even from this distance he was intimidating. Not that he had intimidated *her*, Georgie told herself strongly in the next moment, not a bit of it, but he was one of those men who was uncomfortably, in-your-face male. There was a sort of dark power about him, an aggressive virility that was impossible to ignore, and it was…Georgie searched for the right word and found it. Disturbing. He was disturbing. But he was leaving now and with any luck she would never set eyes on him again.

And then she suddenly realised what she was thinking and offered up a quick urgent prayer of repentance. Robert's whole business, his livelihood, *everything* hung on Matt de Capistrano giving him this contract; how could she—for one second—wish he didn't get it? But she hadn't, she hadn't wished that, she reassured herself frantically the next moment, just that she wouldn't see Matt de Capistrano again. But if Robert got the job—by some miracle—of course she'd have to see him if she continued working here. '*Oh…*' She sighed again, loudly and irritably. The man had got her in such a state she didn't know what she was thinking!

'Well!' Robert opened the door and he was smiling. 'We might, we just might be back in business again.'

'Really?' Georgie forgot all about her dislike of Matt de Capistrano as the naked hope in her brother's face touched her heart. 'He's going to help?'

'Maybe.' Robert was clearly trying to keep a hold on his optimism but he couldn't disguise his relief as he said, 'He's not dismissed it out of hand anyway. It all depends on that phone call tonight and then we'll know one way or the other. He's going to make some enquiries. I can't blame him; I'd do the same in his shoes.'

'Enquiries?' Georgie raised fine arched eyebrows. 'With whom?'

'Anyone he damn well wants,' Robert answered drily. 'I've given him a host of names and numbers—the bank manager, my accountant, firms we've dealt with recently and so on—and told him I'll ring them and tell them to let him have any information he wants. This is my last hope, Georgie. If the man tells me to jump through hoops I'll turn cartwheels as well for good measure.'

'Oh, Robert.' She didn't want him to lose everything, she didn't, but to be rescued by Matt de Capistrano! And it was only in that moment she fully acknowledged the extent of the antagonism which had leapt into immediate life the moment she had laid eyes on the darkly handsome face. She didn't know him, she'd barely exchanged more than a dozen words with him, and yet she disliked him more intensely than anyone else she had ever met. Well, almost anyone. Her thoughts touched on Glen before she closed that particular door in her mind.

'So, cross your fingers and your toes and anything else it's physically possible to cross,' Robert said more quietly now, a nervous note creeping in as they stared at each other. 'If it's no we're down the pan, Georgie; even the house is mortgaged up to the hilt so the kids won't even have a roof over their heads.'

'They will.' Georgie's voice was fierce. 'We'll make sure of that and we'll all stay together too.' But a little grotty flat somewhere wouldn't be the same as Robert's pleasant semi with its big garden and the tree-house he had built for the children a couple of years ago. They had lost their mother and all the security she had embodied; were they going to have to lose their home too?

'Maybe.' And then as Georgie eyed him determinedly Robert smiled as he said, 'Definitely! But let's hope it won't come to uprooting the kids, Georgie. Look, get the bank on the phone for me first, would you? I need to put them and everyone else in the know and explain they'll be getting a call from de Capistrano's people. I don't want anyone else to tread on his very wealthy and powerful toes.'

Georgie looked sharply at Robert at that, and was relieved to see he was grinning at her. 'I'm sorry about what I said,' she said weakly. 'I didn't know he was there. I nearly died when I saw him.'

'You and me both.' Robert shook his head slowly. 'I'd forgotten there's never a dull moment around you, little sister.'

'Oh, you.'

The rest of the day sped by in a flurry of phone-calls, faxes and hastily typed letters, and by the end of the afternoon Georgie was sick of the very sound of Matt de Capistrano's name. Yesterday her life had been difficult—juggling her new role as surrogate mum, cook and housekeeper, Robert's secretary and shoulder to cry on wasn't easy—but today a tall, obnoxious stranger had made it downright impossible, she thought crossly just before five o'clock. Robert had been like a cat on a hot tin roof all day and neither of them had been able to eat any lunch.

One thing had solidified through the hectic afternoon, though. If Matt de Capistrano bailed them out she was leaving here as soon as she could fix up a good secretary for Robert. She could get heaps more money working at temping anyway, and every little bit would help the family budget for the time being. And temping meant she could be there for the children if either of them were ill, without worrying Robert would be struggling at the office, and she could pick and choose when she worked. She might even be able to do a little freelance advertising work if she took a few days out to tote her CV and examples of her artwork designs round the area.

Her previous job, as a designer working on tight deadlines and at high speed for an independent design studio situated north of Watford had been on the other side of London—Robert's house and business being in Sevenoaks—but there were other studios and other offices.

Whatever, she would remove herself from any chance of bumping into Matt de Capistrano. Georgie nodded to the thought, her hands pausing on the keyboard of her word processor as she gazed into space, only to jump violently as the telephone on her desk rang shrilly.

She glanced at her wristwatch as she reached for the receiver. Five o'clock. Exactly. It was him! She ignored the ridiculous churning in her stomach and breathed deeply, her voice steady and cool as she said, 'Millett's Builders. How can I help you?'

'Miss Millett?' The deep voice trickled over her taut nerves gently but with enough weight to make them twang slightly. 'Matt de Capistrano. Is your brother there?'

'Yes, Mr de Capistrano, he's been waiting for your call,' Georgie said briskly.

'Thank you.'

Boy, with a voice like that he'd be dynamite on the silver screen—Sean Connery eat your heart out! Georgie thought flusteredly as she buzzed Robert and put the call through. Deep and husky with the faint accent making it heart-racingly sexy— And then she caught her errant ramblings firmly, more than a little horrified at the way her mind had gone. He was a hateful man, despicable. End of story.

She heard the telephone go down in the other office and when, a moment later, the interconnecting door opened with a flourish she knew. Even before Robert spoke his beaming face told her what the outcome of Matt de Capistrano's enquiries had been. They were in business.

CHAPTER TWO

'WE MEET again, Miss Millett.' In spite of the fact that
Georgie had been steeling herself all morning for this en-
counter, her head snapped up so sharply she felt a muscle
in her neck twang.

A full week had elapsed since that day in Robert's office
when she had first seen Matt de Capistrano, and it was now
the first day of May and a beautiful sunny morning outside
the building. Inside Georgie felt the temperature had just
dropped about ten degrees as she met the icy grey eyes
watching her so intently from the doorway.

'Good morning, Mr de Capistrano.' There was no designer suit today; he was dressed casually in black denim
jeans and a pale cream shirt and if anything the dark aura
surrounding him was enhanced tenfold. Georgie knew he
and Robert were going on site for most of the day, along
with Matt de Capistrano's architects and a whole host of
other people, but she hadn't bargained for what the open-
necked shirt and black jeans which sat snugly on lean male
hips would do to her equilibrium. She wanted to swallow
nervously but she just knew the grey gaze would pick up
the action, and so she said, a little throatily, 'Robert is
waiting for you if you'd like to go through?' as she indicated her brother's office with a wave of her hand.

'Thank you, but I wish to have a word with you first.'

Oh, help! He was going to come down on her like a ton
of bricks for her rudeness a week ago. He held all the cards
and he knew it. He could make their lives hell if he wanted.
Georgie raised her small chin a fraction and her voice be-

23

trayed none of her inward agitation as she looked into the dark attractive face and said quietly, 'Yes, Mr de Capistrano?'

Her little cubby-hole, which was barely big enough to hold her desk and chair and the filing cabinet, and barely warranted the grand name of an office, was covered by one male stride, and then he was standing at the side of her as he said, 'Firstly, I do not think it appropriate we stand on ceremony with the Mr de Capistrano and Miss Millett now we are working together, yes?'

In spite of his perfect English he sounded very foreign. Georgie just had to take that swallow before she could say, 'If that's what you want, Mr de Capistrano.'

'It is,' he affirmed softly. 'And the name is Matt.'

The grey eyes were so dark as to be almost black, Georgie thought inconsequentially, and surrounded by such thick black lashes it seemed a shame to waste them on a man. And he seemed even bigger than she remembered. 'Then please call me Georgie,' she managed politely.

He inclined his head briefly. 'And the second thing is that I find myself in need of your assistance today, Georgie,' he continued smoothly. 'My secretary, Pepita, has unfortunately had a slight accident this morning and twisted her ankle. Perhaps you would take her place on site and take notes for me?'

Oh, no. No, no, no. She'd never survive a day in his company without making a fool of herself or something. She couldn't, she really couldn't do this! If nothing else this confirmed she was doing absolutely the right thing in trying to find a new secretary to take her place for Robert.

Georgie called on every bit of composure she could muster and said steadily, 'Perhaps you had better ask Robert about that. It would mean closing the office here, of course, which is not ideal. His men are finishing work on a shop we've been renovating and are expected to call in some time this afternoon, and there's the phone to answer and so on.'

'You have an answering machine?' Matt enquired pleasantly.

'Yes, but—'

'And your presence will only be required during the discussions with the architect and planner. After that you may return here and perhaps type up the notes for me,' he continued silkily.

Oh, hell! It would be today his precious secretary decided to twist her ankle, Georgie thought helplessly. She doubted if Matt de Capistrano would be around much in the normal run of things; a wealthy tycoon like him had his fingers in a hundred and one pies at any one time, and within a few weeks she would hopefully be out of here anyway. This was *just* the sort of situation she'd been trying to avoid when she'd decided to find a replacement secretary for Robert. 'Well, like I said, you'd best discuss this with Robert,' she said faintly.

'And if Robert agrees? I can tell him you have no objection, yes?' he persisted.

No, no and triple no. 'Of course, Mr—Matt,' Georgie said calmly.

'Thank you, Georgie.'

His accent gave her name emphasis on the last 'e' and lifted it into something quite different from the mundane, and she was just coping with what that did to her nerves when the hard gaze narrowed as he said conversationally, 'You do not like me, Georgie.'

It was a statement, not a question, but even if it had been otherwise Georgie would have been unable to answer him immediately such was the state of her surprise.

'This is not a problem,' he continued smoothly as she

stared at him wide-eyed. His gaze rested briefly on the dark gold of her hair, which hung to her shoulders in a silky bob, before he added, 'Unless you make it one, of course.'

'I... That is—' She was spluttering, she realised suddenly, and with the knowledge came a flood of angry adrenaline that strengthened her voice as her mind became clearer. If he thought she was some pathetic little doormat who would let him walk all over her just because he was bailing them out, he'd got another think coming! She was no one's whipping boy. 'I have no intention of making it one,' she answered smartly.

'This is good.'

Georgie's soft mouth tightened further as she caught what she was sure was the hint of laughter in the dark voice, although his face was betraying no amusement whatsoever, and she struggled to keep her tone even and cool as she said, 'In fact, I don't expect to be working for Robert much longer, actually. It's far better that he has someone else working for him here so that I can divide my time between looking after the children and temping work. So I doubt our paths will cross after that.'

To her absolute horror he sat down on a corner of the desk, his body warmth reaching into her air space as he said quietly, 'Ah, yes, the children. How old are they? Are they coping?'

That same expensive and utterly delicious smell she'd caught wafting off the hard tanned body before was doing wicked things to her hormones, but Georgie was pleased to note nothing of her inward turmoil showed in her voice as she answered evenly, 'The twins are seven, coming up for eight, and they are coping pretty well on the whole. They have lots of friends and their teacher at school at the moment is actually Sandra's—their mother's—best friend, so she is being an absolute brick.'

'And your brother?' he asked quietly, his head tilting as he moved a fraction closer which made her heartbeat quicken. 'How is he doing?'

Georgie cleared her throat. There were probably a million and one men who could sit on her desk all day if they so wished without her turning a hair and without one stray thought coming into her mind. Matt de Capistrano was not one of them.

'Robert is naturally devastated,' she said even more quietly than he had spoken. 'Sandra was his world. They'd known each other since they were children and after they married they even worked together, so their lives were intrinsically linked.'

'I see.' He nodded slowly, and Georgie wondered if he was aware of just how sexy he looked when he narrowed his eyes like that. 'Such devotion is unusual, one might even say exceptional in this day and age of supermarket marriage.'

'Supermarket marriage?' she asked bewilderedly.

'One samples one brand for a while before purchasing another and then another,' he drawled in cynical explanation. 'The lawyers get fatter than anyone, of course.'

'Not all marriages are like that,' Georgie objected steadily. 'Some people fall in love and it lasts a lifetime.'

The grey eyes fastened even more piercingly on her face and now the metallic glint was mocking. 'Don't tell me you are a romantic,' he said derisively.

She had been, once. 'No, I am not a romantic.' Her voice was cool now, and dismissive. 'But I know what Sandra and Robert had was real, that's all.'

She couldn't read the expression on his face now, but as he opened his mouth to speak Robert chose that moment to open the door of his office, his face breaking into a warm smile as he said, 'I thought I heard voices out here. Come on in, Matt. There's just a couple of points I'd like to discuss before we leave.'

Whew! As the door closed behind the two men Georgie slumped in her chair for a moment, one hand smoothing a wisp of silky hair from her flushed face. Something gave her the impression this was going to be one of those days!

She had been banking on using the time the office was quiet with Robert on site to organize the arrangements for the twins' birthday party. She and Robert had suddenly realised the night before that the children's birthday was only a couple of weeks away and neither of them had given it a thought. Sandra had always made a big deal of their birthday and Georgie wanted to keep everything as normal as she could in the circumstances, so—Robert being unable to face the thought of the house being invaded by family and friends and loads of screaming infants—she had thought of booking a hall somewhere and hiring a bouncy castle and a magician and the full works.

The buzzer on her desk interrupted further musing. 'Georgie?' Robert's voice sounded strained. 'Could you organise coffee, make it three cups, would you, and bring in your notebook? I want you to sit in on this.'

What now? Georgie thought as she quickly fetched out the best mugs and a packet of the delicious chocolate caramel biscuits her brother loved. He had lost a great deal of weight in the last months and she had been trying to feed him up since she'd come home.

Once the coffee was ready she straightened her pencil-slim skirt and demure, buttoned-up-to-the-collar blouse and steeled herself for the moment she faced those piercing grey eyes again. Since her first day of working for Robert she had always dressed well, bearing in mind that she was the first impression people received when they walked through the door, but today she had taken extra care and it was only in this moment she acknowledged the fact. And it irritated her. Irritated and annoyed her. She didn't *want* to care what Matt de Capistrano thought of her. He was just a brief fleeting shadow in her life, totally unimportant. *He was.*

The brief and totally unimportant shadow was sitting with one knee over the other and muscled arms stretched along the back of the big comfy visitor's seat in Robert's office when she entered, and immediately her body's re-action to the overt male pose forced her to recognise her own awareness of him. Georgie was even more ruffled when her innate honesty emphasised that his flagrant mas-culinity was all the more overwhelming for its casual un-consciousness, and after serving the men their coffee and offering them the plate of biscuits she sat down herself, folding her hands neatly in her lap after placing her own coffee within easy reach. She was not going to fidget or gabble or react in any way to Matt de Capistrano, not if it killed her.

'So...' Robert's voice was still strained. 'To recap, you feel Mains and Jenson will have to go?' he said to Matt, referring to the two elderly bricklayers who had been with Robert since he first started the firm fourteen years ago.

'What?' Georgie forgot all about the non-reaction as she reared up in her seat. 'George and Walter?' She had known the two men even before she had come under Robert's wing and they had always treated her like a favourite grand-daughter, as had their wives. The first summer she had come to live with Robert and Sandra, when she'd been bitterly grieving for her parents, Walter and his wife had taken her away to France for two weeks to try and take her mind off her parents' untimely death and they had been utterly wonderful to her. 'You can't! You can't get rid of them.'

'Excuse me?' The steel-grey eyes had narrowed into slits of light and he was frowning.

'They're like family,' Georgie said passionately.

'Family's fine,' Matt said coolly. 'Inefficient employees are something else. Walter Jenson is well past retiring age and George Mains turned sixty-five a year ago.'

'They are excellent bricklayers!' Her green eyes were flashing sparks now.

'They are too slow,' he said dismissively, 'and this is not a charitable concern for geriatrics. Your brother must have lost thousands over the last few years by carrying men like Mains and Jenson. I've no doubt of their experience or the quality of their work, but Jenson was off sick more than he was at work over the last twelve months—severe arthritis, isn't it?' he asked in a brief aside to Robert, who nodded unhappily. 'And Mains's unfortunate stroke last year has slowed him up to the point where I believe he actually represents something of a danger to himself and others, especially when working on scaffolding. If you drop something from any sort of height you could kill or maim anyone beneath.'

'I don't believe this!' She glared at him angrily. 'They are craftsmen, the pair of them.'

'They are old craftsmen and it's time to let some young blood take over,' Matt said ruthlessly, 'however much it hurts.'

'And of course it really hurts you, doesn't it?' Georgie bit out furiously, ignoring Robert's frantic hand-signals as she jerked to her feet. 'Two dear ol—' She caught herself as the grey gaze sharpened. 'Two dear men who have been the rocks on which this business was built just thrown on to the scrap heap. What reward is that for all their faithfulness to Robert and this family? But faithfulness means nothing to men like you, does it? You've made your millions, you're sitting pretty, but you're still greedy for more and if more means men like Walter and George get sacrificed along the way then so be it.'

'Have you quite finished?' He was still sitting in the relaxed manner of earlier but the grey gaze was lethal and pointed straight at Georgie's flushed face. 'Then sit down, Miss Millett.'

'I don't think—'

'*Sit down!*'

The bark made her jump and in spite of herself Georgie felt her legs obey him.

'Firstly, your brother has made it clear just what he owes these two employees and they will be retired with a very generous package,' Matt ground out coldly. 'I think, as does Robert if he speaks the truth, that this will not come as a surprise to them; neither will it be wholly displeasing. Secondly, you talk of sacrifice when you are prepared to jeopardise the rest of your brother's employees' livelihoods for the sake of two elderly men who should have retired years ago?

'It is human nature for the rest of the men to tailor their speed to the slowest worker when there is a set wage at the end of each week. Your brother's workers have been underachieving for years and a week ago they were in danger of reaping their reward, every one of them. If Robert had gone bankrupt everyone would have been a loser. There is no place for weakness in industry; you should know that.'

'And kindness?' She continued to glare at him even though a tiny part of her brain was pressing her to recognise there was more than an element of truth in what he had said. 'What about kindness and gratitude? How do you think they'll feel at being told they're too old?'

'They know the dates on their birth certificates as well

as anyone,' he said icily, 'so I doubt it will come as the surprise you seem to foresee.'

He folded his arms over his chest, settling more comfortably in his seat as he studied her stiff body and tense face through narrowed eyes.

Georgie didn't respond immediately, more because she was biting back further hot words as the full portent of what she had yelled at him registered than because she was intimidated by his coldness. And then she said, her voice shaking slightly, 'I think what you are demanding Robert do is awful.'

'Then don't think.' He sat forward in his seat, draining his mug with one swallow and turning to Robert as he said, 'I'd suggest you take this opportunity to change the men over to piece work. With a set goal each week and good bonuses for extra achievement you'll soon sort out the wheat from the chaff, and you've limped on long enough.'

Georgie looked at her brother, willing him to stand up to this tyrant, but Robert merely nodded thoughtfully. 'I'd been thinking along the same lines myself,' he agreed quietly.

'Good, that's settled, then,' Matt said imperturbably. 'Now, if you'd like to get Georgie to note those few points that need checking on site we'll be on our way. Have you got any other shoes than those?' he added, looking at her wafer-thin high heels which she had never worn to the office before but which went perfectly with the charcoal skirt she was wearing. They also showed her legs—which Georgie considered her best feature, hating her small bust and too-slender hips—off to their best advantage, but she'd tried to excuse that thought all morning.

Georgie was still mentally reeling from the confrontation of the last few minutes, and a full ten seconds went by before she could say, her voice suitably cutting, 'I wasn't aware I was expected to go on site this morning, if you remember, so, no, I haven't any other shoes with me.'

'There's your wellies in the back of my car,' Robert put in helpfully. 'You remember we put all our boots in there when we took the kids down to the river for that walk at the weekend?'

Her brother probably had no idea why she glared at him the way she did, Georgie reflected, as she said, 'Thank you, Robert,' in a very flat voice. She was going to look just great, wasn't she? Expensive silk jade-green blouse, elegant skirt and great hefty black wellington boots. Wonderful. And that...that *swine* sitting there so complacently with his hateful grey eyes looking her up and down was to blame for this, and he was enjoying every minute of her discomfiture. She didn't have to look at him to know that; it was radiating out from the lean male figure in waves.

As it happened, by the time Georgie jumped out of Robert's old car at the site of the proposed new estate she wasn't thinking about her appearance.

Newbottle Meadow, as the site had always been called by all the children thereabouts, was old farmland and still surrounded by grazing cattle in the far distance. When Georgie had first come to live with her brother and his wife the area had been virtually country, but the swiftly encroaching urban advance had swallowed hundreds of acres and now Newbottle Meadow was on the edge of the town. But as yet it was still unspoilt and beautiful.

Georgie stood gazing at the rolling meadowland filled with pink-topped grasses and buttercups and butterflies and she wanted to cry. According to Robert, Matt de Capistrano had had the foresight to buy the land a decade ago when it had still officially been farmland. After several appeals he had managed to persuade the powers-that-be to grant his application for housing—as he had known would happen eventually—thereby guaranteeing a thousandfold profit as relatively inexpensive agricultural land became prime development ground. And then with the yuppie-style estate he was proposing to build...

Philistine! Georgie gulped in the mild May sunshine which turned the buttercups to luminescent gold and the grasses to pink feathers, and forced back the tears pricking the backs of her eyes. Badgers lived here, along with rabbits and foxes and butterflies galore. She and her friends had spent many happy hours marching out of the town to the meadow where they had camped for days on end and had a whale of a time. And now it was all going to be ripped up—mutilated—for filthy lucre. But it would be the saving of Robert's firm and ultimately her brother himself. The blow of losing his business as well as his wife would have been horrific.

Georgie bit hard on her lip as she turned to see Matt de Capistrano's red Lamborghini—obviously the Mercedes and the chauffeur were having a day off!—glide to a silky-smooth stop a few yards away. She had to think of Robert and the children in all of this, she told herself fiercely. Her ideals, the unspoilt meadow and all the wildlife, weren't as important as David and Annie and Robert.

'You could turn milk sour with that face.'

'What?' She was so startled by the softly drawled insult as Matt reached her side that she literally gaped at him.

'Forget Mains and Jenson; the decision has been made,' Matt said quietly, his eyes roaming to Robert, who had joined the other men waiting for them in the middle of the acres of meadowland.

'I wasn't thinking about George and Walter,' she returned without thinking.

'No?' He eyed her disbelievingly.

'No.''

''Then what?' he asked softly, turning to look into her heart-shaped face. 'Why the ferocious glare and wishing me six foot under?'

'I wasn't—' She stopped abruptly in the middle of the denial. Maybe she had been at that. But he would never understand in a million years, besides which she would be cutting off her nose—or Robert's nose—to spite her face if she did or said anything to stop Robert securing this contract. Matt de Capistrano would simply use another builder and the estate would become reality anyway. 'It doesn't matter,' she finished weakly.

'Georgie.' Before she could object he had turned her round, his hand lifting her chin as he looked down into the green of her eyes. 'Tell me. I'm a big boy. I can take it.'

It was the mockery that did it. He was laughing at her again and Georgie stiffened, her eyes slanting green fire as she fairly spat, 'You're going to spoil this beautiful land, desecrate it, and you just don't care, do you? You've got no soul.'

For a moment he just stared at her in amazement, and she observed—with a shred of satisfaction in all the pain and embarrassment—that she had managed to shock him. 'What?' he growled quietly.

'I used to play here as a child, camp out with my friends and have fun,' she said tightly. 'And this land is still one of the few places hereabouts which is truly wild and beautiful. People come here to *breathe*, don't you see? And you are going to destroy it, along with all the wildlife and the beauty—'

'People have been allowed to come here because I didn't stop them,' he said impatiently. 'I could have fenced it off but I didn't.'

'Because it was too much trouble,' she shot back quickly.

'For crying out loud!' He stared at her with very real incredulity. 'Is there no end to my crimes where you are concerned? Don't you want Robert to build this estate?'

'Of course I do.' She stared at him angrily. 'And I don't. Of course I don't! How could I when I look at all this and think that in a few months it will be covered with bulldozers and dirt and pretty little houses for people who think the latest designer label and a Mercedes are all that matters in life? But I don't want Robert to lose his chance of making good; I love him and he's worked so hard and been through so much. So of course I want him to have the contract.'

He shut his eyes for a moment in a way that said far more than any words could have done, and she resented him furiously for the unspoken criticism and the guilt it engendered. She was being ridiculous, illogical and totally unreasonable, but she couldn't help it. She just couldn't help it. This meadowland had healed something deep inside her in the terrible aftermath of her parents' death. The peace, the tranquillity, the overriding *continuing* of life here had meant so much. And now it was all going to be swept away.

It had welcomed her after the Glen episode in her life too, reaching out to her with comforting fingers as she had walked the childhood paths and let her fingers brush through grasses and wild flowers that had had an endless consistency about them in a world that had suddenly been turned upside down.

'I'm sorry.' Suddenly all the anger had seeped away and she felt she had shrunk down to a child again. 'This isn't your fault, not altogether.'

He said something in Spanish that she was sure was uncomplimentary, then said in English, 'Thank you, Georgie.

That makes me feel a whole lot better,' in tones of deep and biting sarcasm.

'You won't take the contract from Robert because you are angry with me?' she asked anxiously.

His mouth tightened still more and now the hand under her chin became a vice as he looked down into the emerald orbs staring up at him. 'I think I like it better when you are aware you are insulting me,' he said very softly.

Under the thin silk shirt she could see a dark shadow and guessed his chest was covered with body hair. He would probably be hairy all over. Somehow it went with the intoxicating male perfume of him, the overall *alienness* of Matt de Capistrano that was threatening and exciting at the same time. And she didn't want to be threatened or excited. She just wanted... What? She didn't know what she wanted any more.

'Georgie?'

She heard Robert calling through the buzzing in her ears as the warm hand under her chin held her for a second more, his gaze stroking over her bewildered face. And then he let her go, stepping away from her as he called in an unforgivably controlled voice, 'We are just coming, Robert. Georgie has been reminiscing about her childhood up here. It must have been fun.'

Philistine!

CHAPTER THREE

GEORGIE felt it wise to keep a very low profile during the rest of the morning, quietly taking notes on all that was said as she plodded after the men in her flapping wellington boots. She made sure she had no eye contact at all with Matt, even when he spoke directly to her as she found herself walking with him to the parked cars. 'Thank you, Georgie, that's your job here done for today,' he said easily. 'We are going to grab a spot of lunch before we finish off this afternoon. Would you care to join us?'

'I don't think so.' She looked somewhere in the middle of his tanned throat as she said quietly, 'I've things to do back at the office.' The last thing, the very last thing in all the world she wanted to do was to sit in a social atmosphere and make small talk with Matt de Capistrano.

'But surely you will have to eat?' he persisted softly.

'I've brought sandwiches which I'll eat at my desk.'

'How industrious of you.'

Sarcastic swine! 'Not really,' she answered tightly. 'I want to telephone a few places and set up the arrangements for Robert's children's birthday party. It's been pretty busy over the last few weeks and it's only just dawned on us they'll be eight in two weeks' time. We want to make their birthday as special as we can for them.'

He nodded as she forced herself to meet the grey eyes at last. 'What are you planning?' he asked, as though he were really interested.

Which she was sure he wasn't, Georgie thought cynically. Why would a multi-millionaire like Matt de

Capistrano care about two eight-year-olds' birthday party? 'A hall somewhere with a bouncy castle and so on,' she answered dismissively.

'Ah, yes, the bouncy castle.' He looked down at her, his piercing eyes glittering pewter in the sunshine. 'My nephews and nieces enjoy these things too.'

He was an uncle? Ridiculously she was absolutely amazed. Somehow she couldn't picture him as anything other than a cold business tycoon, but of course he would have a family. Robert had mentioned in passing some days ago that Matt de Capistrano was not married, but that didn't stop him being a son or a brother. She brought her racing thoughts under control and said quietly, 'Children are the same everywhere.'

'So it would seem.' He looked at her for a second more before turning to glance at Robert in the distance, who was still deep in conversation with the chief architect. 'I will take you back to the office while the others finish off here and meet them at the pub,' he said expressionlessly.

'No.' It was too quick and too instinctive and they both recognised it. Georgie felt her cheeks begin to burn and said feverishly, 'I mean, I wouldn't want to put you to any trouble and Robert won't mind. Or, better still, I could take his car and he can go with you—'

'It is no trouble, Georgie.' The words themselves were nothing; the manner in which they were said told her all too clearly she had annoyed him again and he was now determined to have his own way. As usual.

Could she refuse to ride with him? Georgie's eyes flickered to Robert's animated face and her brother's excitement was the answer. No, she couldn't. 'If you're sure you don't mind,' she said weakly, striving to act as if this was a perfectly normal conversation instead of one as potentially explosive as a loaded gun.

'Not at all.' He bent close enough for her to scent his male warmth as he said softly but perfectly seriously, 'The pleasure will be all mine.' And he allowed just a long enough pause before he added, 'As we both know.'

This time Georgie couldn't think of a single thing to say, and so she stood meekly at his side as he called to Robert and informed him he would see them all at the White Knight after he had taken Georgie back to the office. Her eyes moved to the red Lamborghini crouching at the side of the road. She had never ridden in a Lamborghini before; in fact she hadn't seen one this close up before either. Perhaps at a different time with a different driver the experience would be one to be savoured, but the car was too like its master to be anything else but acutely disturbing.

It was even more overwhelming when she found herself in the passenger seat and Matt shut the door gently behind her. She felt as though she was cocooned in leather and metal—which she supposed she was—and the car was so low she felt she was sitting on a level with the ground. However, those sensations were nothing to the ones which seized her senses once Matt slid in beside her.

The riot in her stomach was flushing her face, she just knew it was, but she couldn't do a thing about it, and when Matt turned to her and said quietly, but with a throb of amusement in his voice, 'Would you like to take those off?' as he nodded at her boots which were almost reaching her chin she stiffened tensely. How like him to point out she looked ridiculous, she told herself silently. He couldn't have made it more clear he found her totally unattractive. But that was fine; in fact it was great. *Really* great. Because that was exactly how she viewed him.

'No.' She forced herself to glance haughtily his way and then wished with all her heart she hadn't. He was much, much too close.

'I can come round and slip them off for you if it's difficult with that tight skirt?' he offered helpfully.

Georgie felt more trapped than ever. 'No, I'm fine,' she said tightly, staring resolutely out of the windscreen.

'Georgie, it is the middle of the day and I am giving you a lift back to the office,' he said evenly. 'Can't you let yourself relax in my company for just a minute or two? I promise you I have no intention of diverting to a deserted lane somewhere and having my wicked way with you, even if you do view me as a cross between the Marquis de Sade and Adolf Hitler.'

Shocked into looking at him again, she said quickly, 'I didn't think you were and of course I don't think you're like either of those two men!'

'No?' It reeked of disbelief.

'No.' This was awful, terrible. She should never have got into this car.

He raised his eyebrows at her but then to her intense relief he turned, starting the engine, which purred into life with instant obedience.

She turned back to the windscreen, but not before she had noticed the lingering amusement curling the hard mouth. He was obviously enjoying her discomfiture and, more to show him she was completely in control of herself than anything else, Georgie said primly, 'This is a very nice car.'

'Nice?' He reacted as though she had said something unforgivable. 'Georgie, family saloons are *nice*, along with sweet old maiden aunts and visits to the zoo and a whole host of other unremarkable things in this world of ours. A Lamborghini—' he paused just long enough to make his point '—is not in that category.'

She'd annoyed him. Good. It felt great to have got under that inch-thick skin. 'Well, that's how I see it,' she said sweetly. 'A car is just a car, after all, a lump of metal to get you quickly from A to B. A functional necessity.'

'I'm not even going to reply to that.'

She saw him glance down at the leather steering wheel and the beautiful dashboard as though to reassure himself that his pride and joy was still as fabulous as he thought it was, and she repressed a smile. Okay, she was probably being mean but, as he'd said earlier, he was a big boy; he could take it. 'I'm sorry if I've offended you,' she lied quietly.

'Sure you are.' The husky, smoky voice caught at her nerve-ends and she allowed herself another brief peek at the hard profile. He had rolled the sleeves of his shirt up at some point during the morning and his muscled arms, liberally covered with a dusting of black silky hair, swam into view. His shirt collar was open and several buttons undone and his shoulders were very broad. His body had an aggressive, top-heavy maleness that was impossible for any female to ignore.

The incredible car, the man driving it so effortlessly, the bright May sunshine slanting through the trees lining the road down which they were travelling—it was all the stuff dreams were made of, Georgie thought to herself a touch hysterically. He was altogether larger than life, Matt de Capistrano, and he was totally unaware of it.

'Are both the Mercedes and this car yours?' she asked carefully after a full minute had crept by in a screaming silence that had become more uncomfortable second by second.

'Would that be a further nail in my coffin?'

The very English phrase, spoken in the dark accented voice and without a glance at her, caused Georgie to stiffen slightly. 'I don't know what you mean,' she said flatly.

'I think you do,' he returned just as flatly.

'Now, look—' Whatever she had been about to say ended in a squeak as he pulled the car into the side of the road and cut the engine. 'What are you doing?' she asked nervously.

'I want to look at you while I talk to you,' he said softly, 'that is all, so do not panic, little English mouse.'

'Mouse?' He couldn't have said anything worse, and then, as she jerked to face him and saw the smile twisting the firm lips, she knew he was teasing her.

And then the smile faded as he said, 'I think we need to get a few things out into the open, Georgie.'

'Do we?' She didn't think so. She *really* didn't think so. And certainly not here, in this sumptuous car with him about an inch away and with nowhere to run to. She should never have antagonised him, she acknowledged much too late.

'You look on me as the enemy and this is not the case at all,' Matt said softly. 'If your brother fails, I fail. If he makes good, it's good news for me too.'

The hostility which had flared into life the minute she had set eyes on him, and which showed no signs of abating, was nothing to do with Robert and all to do with her, Georgie thought as she stared into the metallic grey eyes narrowed against the sunlight. But she could hardly say that, could she? So instead she managed fairly calmly, 'I think that's stretching credulity a little far. This business is everything Robert has; your interest here is just a tiny drop in the vast ocean of your business empire. It would hardly dent your coffers if this whole project went belly up.'

'I have never had a business venture go "belly up", as you so charmingly put it, and I do not intend for your brother's to be the first,' Matt returned smoothly. 'Besides which…'

He paused, and Georgie said, 'Yes?'

'Besides which, you underestimate his assets,' Matt said quietly.

'I can assure you I do not,' Georgie objected. 'Robert has no secrets from me and—'

'I wasn't talking about financial assets, Georgie.'

'Then what?' She stared at him, her clear sea-green eyes reflecting her bewilderment.

He had stretched one arm along the back of her seat as he turned to face her after switching off the engine, and she was so aware of every little inch of him that she was as tense as piano wire. It wasn't that she expected him to jump on her—Robert had told her it was common knowledge Matt de Capistrano had women, beautiful, gorgeous women, chasing after him all the time and that he could afford to pick and choose—more that she didn't trust herself around him. She seemed destined to meet him head-on and usually ended up making a fool of herself in the process. He was such an *unsettling* individual.

'What do you mean?' she repeated after a moment or two when he continued to look at her, his eyes with their strange dark-silver hue holding her own until everything else around them was lost in the intensity of his gaze.

'He has you.' It was soft and silky, and Georgie floundered.

'Me?' She tried for a laugh to lighten what had become a painfully protracted conversation but it turned into more of a squeak.

'Yes, you.' He wasn't touching her, in fact he hadn't moved a muscle, but suddenly he had taken her into an intimacy that was absorbing and Georgie found herself thinking, If he can make me feel like this, here, in the middle of the day and without any desire on his part, what on earth is he like with those women he does desire? No

wonder they flock round him. As a lover he must be pure
dynamite.

And that shocked her into saying, 'Sometimes I'm more
of a liability than an asset, as you well know,' her voice
over-bright.

'I know nothing of the sort. How can honesty and ide-
alism be viewed in that way?' he returned quietly.

She wished he would stop looking at her. She wished he
would start the car again. She wished she had never agreed
to have this lift with him in the first place! 'You don't agree
with me about Newbottle Meadow for a start.' She forced
an aggressiveness she didn't really feel as an instinctive
protection against her body's response to his closeness.

'I don't have to agree with you to admire certain qualities
inherent in your make-up,' he returned softly.

'No, I suppose not,' she agreed faintly, deciding if she
went along with him he would be satisfied he had made
his point—whatever that was—and they could be on their
way again.

He gave her a hard look. 'Don't patronise me, Georgie.'

'Patronise you?' She bristled instantly. 'I wouldn't dream
of patronising you!'

The frown beetling his eyebrows faded into a quizzical
ruffle. 'But you enjoy challenging me, don't you?' he murmured in a softly provoking voice that stiffened Georgie's
back. 'Do you know why you like doing that?' he added
in a tone that stated quite clearly he knew exactly what
motivated her.

Because you are an egotistical, unfeeling, condescend-
ing—

He interrupted her thoughts, his voice silky smooth. 'Because you are sexually attracted to me and you're fighting
it in a manner as old as time,' he stated with unforgivable
coolness.

For a moment she couldn't believe he had actually said what she thought he had said, and then she shut her mouth, which had fallen open, before opening it again to snap, 'It might be hard for you to accept, Mr de Capistrano, but not every female you look at feels the need to swoon at your feet!' as she glared at him hotly.

'I can accept that perfectly well,' he returned easily, 'but I'm talking about you, not anyone else.' His expression was totally impassive, which made their conversation even more incredible in Georgie's eyes. The colossal *ego* of the man, she thought wildly. 'And I know I'm right because I feel the same way; I want you more than I've wanted a woman in a long time. For however long it lasted it would be good between us.'

Georgie fumbled with the door handle. 'I'm not listening to this rubbish a second longer,' she ground out through clenched teeth, more to stop her voice shaking than anything else.

'You are going to look slightly...unusual walking through town with your present attire, are you not?' Matt asked evenly as he glanced at the acres of rubber adorning her feet. 'And there is no need to be embarrassed, Georgie. You want me, I want you—it is the most natural thing in the world. There's even a rumour it's what makes it go round. It doesn't have to be complicated.'

The amusement in the dark face was the last straw. She turned on him like a small green-eyed cat, her eyes spitting sparks as she shouted, 'You are actually daring to proposition me? In cold blood?'

'Oh, is that what the matter is?' His expression was hard to read now but she thought it was cynicism twisting the ruthless mouth. 'You wanted a bouquet of red roses and promises of undying love and for everness? Sorry, but I don't believe in either.'

'I didn't want anything!'

'Then why are you so upset?' he asked reasonably. 'You could just tell me I've got it wrong without the melodrama, surely? It's not the most dreadful thing in the world to be told you are desirable by a member of the opposite sex.'

Desirable. Matt de Capistrano thought she was desirable and, if she hadn't got all this horribly wrong, he had been suggesting they have an affair. Georgie felt a churning in her stomach that wasn't all fury, and it was only in that moment she acknowledged Matt knew her better than she knew herself. But she would die before she let him know that, she added with deadly resolve.

'There are ways and ways of being told something,' she said tightly, hearing the prim-sounding words with something of a mental wince.

'I thought you appreciated honesty.'

'I do!' She glared at him, furiously angry that he was trying to make her feel bad about objecting to his stark proposal.

'Let's just test that statement, shall we?' he suggested silkily, and before she could object she found herself in his arms. The kiss was as devastating as ever she had imagined—and she *had* imagined what it would be like to be held in his arms like this, she admitted silently. It was sweet and knowing and erotic, and the feel of him, the intoxicating exhilaration which was inflaming her senses and making her head spin, was irresistible.

Matt was breathing hard, his muscled body rigid as he held her to him in the narrow confines of the car, and the gentle eroticism was a conscious assault on her senses. Georgie knew that. But somehow—and this was even more frightening than the sensations his lovemaking was calling forth—somehow she couldn't find the strength to resist him.

If he had used his superior strength and tried to force her, even slightly, she might have objected. But he was a brilliant strategist. Even that thought was without power compared to the tumultuous emotions flooding her from the top of her head to the soles of her feet.

He was holding her lightly but firmly, one hand tilting her chin to give his mouth greater access to hers, and slowly but subtly his mouth and tongue were growing more insistent. She didn't want to kiss him back and she knew she mustn't, but somehow that was exactly what she was doing. Which didn't make any sense, her struggling thoughts told her feverishly. But then what did sense have to do with Matt de Capistrano?

Everything! Now her mind was screaming the warning. Everything, and she forgot it at her peril. A man like him wouldn't be interested in a girl like her for more than two minutes. She had sparked his attention because she had stood up to him—insulted him, actually—and that was all. It would be a fleeting episode in the life of a very busy man; remembered one moment and then forgotten for ever. *But she wouldn't be able to forget it.*

When she jerked away from him he made no effort at all to restrain her, which to Georgie was further proof of the strength of his interest. He saw her as a brief dalliance, she thought wildly. Wham, bam and thank you, ma'am, while this project was on the go and he had to be around now and again, and then he would be off to pastures new without a second thought.

'I don't want to do this,' she said feverishly, straining back against the passenger door as she stared into the dark face and the piercingly grey eyes fixed on her flushed face.

He said nothing for a moment, his expression unreadable, and then he settled back in his own seat and started the engine again, drawing out on to the road before he said quietly, 'Yes, you do, but you are frightened of the consequences. You needn't be. It would simply be a case of two relative strangers getting to know each other a little better with no strings attached and no heavy commitment.'

Oh, yes, and pigs might fly. However nicely he put it, he wanted her in his bed, and whilst he might be able to engage in sex with 'no strings attached' she could not. She simply wasn't made that way. She breathed in deeply and then out again, calling on her considerable will-power to enable her voice to be calm and steady. 'I don't want to get to know anyone right at the moment, Matt,' she said firmly. 'I have more than enough on my plate with Robert and the children. I neither want nor could cope with anything else.'

'Rubbish.' It was brisk and irritatingly self-assured, and had the effect on Georgie of making her want to lean across and bop him on his arrogant nose.

'It's not rubbish,' she said tightly. 'And we don't even *like* each other, for goodness' sake!' She glanced at him as she spoke, and saw the black brows rise. 'Well, we don't,' she reiterated strongly.

'I like you, Georgie,' he said very evenly.

Okay, plain speaking time! 'You want me in your bed,' she corrected bravely. She heard him draw a quick breath, and added hurriedly, 'And that is something quite different.'

'I can assure you I would not take a woman into my bed whom I did not like,' Matt said calmly. 'All right?'

She wasn't going to win this one. Georgie forced herself not to argue with him and said instead, 'There is no question of my having a relationship with you, Matt, however free-floating.'

They had drawn well into the suburbs now, and as the Lamborghini purred down a main residential street an elegant young woman, complete with obligatory designer shopping bags, stepped straight in front of the car. Matt swore loudly as he braked violently, coming to a halt a foot or so away from the voluptuous redhead, whereupon he wound down the window and asked her, in no uncertain terms, what exactly she was playing at.

Georgie watched as the beautifully made-up face turned his way and a pair of slanted blue eyes surveyed first the car, and then Matt, and she wasn't surprised at the gushing apology which followed, or the suggestion that if there was anything, *anything* she could do to make amends for giving him such a fright he must say.

To be fair Matt didn't appear to notice either the red-head's beauty or her eagerness to make atonement, but no doubt if he had been alone in the car that would have been a different matter, Georgie told herself as they drove on. And this sort of thing would happen a hundred times over, in various forms, to someone like Matt de Capistrano. There would always be a redhead somewhere—or a blonde or brunette—who would let him know they were ready and available.

He was a wealthy, powerful and good-looking man, and the first two attributes made the third literally irresistible to some women. Not that it was just women who were drawn to members of the opposite sex who could guarantee them a life of wealth and ease... Her soft mouth tightened at the thought.

And Matt was a sensual man, dynamic and definitely dangerous. He was as much out of her league as the man in the moon.

'You haven't said a word in five minutes.' The deep cool voice at the side of her made her jump. 'I'll have to kiss you more often if it turns you into a sweet, submissive-type female.'

'I said all there was to say,' she bit back immediately, bristling instantly at the covert suggestion his lovemaking had rendered her weak and fluttery.

'You didn't say anything.' They had just reached the set of traffic lights before they turned into the street in which Robert's premises were situated, and as the lights glowed red Matt brought the car to a halt and glanced at her, his eyes narrowed and disturbingly perceptive. 'Someone has hurt you, haven't they, Georgie?'

She blinked just once, but other than that slight reaction she forced herself to remain absolutely still and keep her expression as deadpan as she could. Nevertheless it was some seconds before she trusted herself to say, with a suitably mocking note in her voice, 'You assume I've been hurt because I don't want to jump into bed with you? Now who's being melodramatic?'

And then the lights changed and the lasers drilling into her brain returned to the windscreen as he drove on. She wanted to sink back in the seat but she kept herself straight, willing herself to think about nothing but exiting from the car in as dignified a manner as possible.

Her lips were still tingling from his kiss, and now she was berating herself for not responding more vigorously to his audacity in thinking he could come on to her like that. She should have made it clear that she considered his effrontery impertinent at the very least, she told herself silently, not entered into a discussion on the pros and cons of having an affair with him! She'd handled this all wrong. But ever since she had got into this sex machine on wheels she had felt intensely vulnerable and more aware of Matt than ever.

They drew up outside Robert's small brick building after Matt had negotiated the Lamborghini carefully into the untidy yard, strewn with all manner of building materials, and before she could move he had opened his door and was walking round the sleek bonnet to hers.

'Thank you.' Emerging gracefully from a Lamborghini clad in the original seven-league boots was not an option, and Georgie was pink-cheeked by the time she was standing. 'I'll type those notes ready for you to collect later,' she said stiffly.

'I've no intention of giving up, Georgie.'

'I beg your pardon?'

He looked down at her from his vantage point of six foot plus, his eyes wandering over her small heart-shaped face and corn-coloured hair, and he brushed one silky strand from her cheek as he said, 'I want you... very much.'

'That... that doesn't mean anything. There must be a hundred and one women out there who are more than willing to jump into bed with you,' she said quickly through the sudden tightness in her chest.

'You've got some sort of fixation about me and bed, haven't you?' It was thoughtful. 'I wonder what Freud would make of that?'

'Now, look, Matt—'

'But I don't mind,' he said kindly. 'You can fantasise about it all you want, but I can assure you when it happens it will be outside all your wildest imaginings.'

'I've told you, it is *not* going to happen!'

She was talking to the air. He had already disappeared round the bonnet of the car and slid into the driver's seat, letting the growling engine have its head as he roared out of the yard with scant regard for other road users.

Georgie stood for some minutes as the dust slowly settled in the golden sunshine and the mild May breeze ruffled her hair with gentle fingers. He frightened her. The thought was there before she could reject it but immediately she rebelled. He didn't. Of course he didn't! Maybe her own reactions to him frightened her, but that was different. She could control them. *She could.* And she would. This time the affirmation in her head was even stronger. Oh, yes, she would all right. She'd had enough of love and romance to last her a lifetime. Once Robert and the children were over the worst, perhaps in a few months, she would put all her energy into the career she had begun on leaving university two years ago, and she would work until she reached every goal she set herself. Autonomous. That was how she wanted to be.

She turned sharply, entering the office and kicking off the boots as though they were the source of all her present troubles. She had the notes to type up and the children's party venue to arrange; she had to get working immediately. The thought was there but still she stood staring out of the window, the incident with Matt evoking a whole host of memories she normally kept under lock and key.

Glen Williams. If she closed her eyes she could picture him easily: tall lean frame, a shock of light brown hair that always fell over his brow in a lopsided quiff, bright blue eyes and a determined square chin. His parents had lived next door to Robert and Sandra and she had met Glen, who was two years older than her, on the first day she had come to live with them, along with his two sisters, one of whom was her age and the other a year younger.

She had immediately become great friends with the two girls, which had been just what she needed at the time, being heartsore and tearful at the loss of her parents, and for the first few years Glen had treated her in the same way he had his kid sisters—teasingly and with some disdain. And then, on her fourteenth birthday, something had changed.

She had dressed up for her birthday disco and had had her waist-length hair cut into a short sleek bob earlier in the day, and from the moment Glen had walked in with a bunch of his pals he had monopolised her. Not that she had minded—she had been consumed with a schoolgirl crush on him for ages. And from that evening they had been inseparable and very much an official 'item' in their group of friends.

Glen had not been academic but had always had a passion for motor cars. After failing every one of his A levels, he had used his considerable charm and got taken on at a local car supermarket-type garage in the town as a trainee mechanic.

That same year she had achieved mostly As in her GCSEs, and had gone on to attain two As and a B in her A levels two years later. During those years they had spent every spare moment they could together and had had some wonderful times, even though they hadn't had two pennies to rub together.

Georgie continued to stare out of the window but now she was blind and deaf to anything but the memories swamping her consciousness.

Glen had been so encouraging when she had tentatively discussed embarking on an Art and Design degree. She would come home weekends—he'd come and fetch her himself—and with him doing so well at the garage and Georgie sure to qualify well and get a great job, they'd be set up for the future. Nice house with a garden, holidays abroad and later the requisite two point four children. They'd got it all worked out—or so she had thought.

And so she had happily trotted off to university with Glen's ring on the third finger of her left hand—he had proposed the night before she had left—and for the first little while everything had seemed fine. He had arrived to collect her each weekend and they had planned a small register office wedding—all they could afford—at

Christmas. She would be nearly nineteen then and Glen had just had his twenty-first birthday. His parents had offered to convert Glen's big double bedroom into a little bedsit by adding a two-seater sofa, small fridge and microwave to the three-quarter-size bed, TV and video and wardrobe the room already contained, as their wedding present, and Robert and Sandra's gift had been a proposed two-week holiday in the sun. They would be together every weekend in their snug little nest and once she had finished her degree and got a job they would think about looking for a house. Life had been cut and dried.

It had been round about the end of November she'd really noticed the change in him. The last couple of weekends she had felt he was distant, cool even, but he had just been promoted at work and she had put his remoteness down to the added responsibility and pressure. The problem had been work all right—but the owner's daughter, not Glen's new position.

Harold Bloomsbury owned a string of garages across London and the south east and his only daughter was the original pampered darling. Julia had made up her mind she wanted Glen—Georgie had later found out she had been flirting with him for ages on and off, but when Glen had got engaged Julia's pursuit had become serious—and although she was plump and plain the Bloomsburys' lifestyle was anything but Spartan. Magnificent townhouse and a villa in Tuscany and another in Barbados, along with a yacht and fast cars and all the trimmings of wealth—Julia's husband would be guaranteed a life of comfort and ease by daddy-in-law.

Glen had weighed all that on the one side and love in a tiny bedsit in his parents' house on the other, and three weeks before they were due to get married had told her the wedding was off. He hadn't said a word about Julia;

Georgie had found out about the other girl through a friend of a friend a few days later. They were too young to settle down, he had lied, and he'd felt it was being terribly unfair to her to get married whilst she was doing her degree. They had lived in each other's pockets for five years—perhaps it was time for a break to see how they both felt? Maybe at Easter they could meet and review the situation and go from there?

She had been stunned and bewildered, Georgie remembered now as she turned abruptly from the window and gazed at her desk piled high with paperwork. She had cried and—this made her stomach curl in recollection—had begged Glen to reconsider. He'd been her life for years; she hadn't been able to imagine a world in which he didn't have pre-eminence.

For a week she had been sunk in misery and unable to eat or sleep, and then she'd found out about Bloomsbury's daughter and her ex-fiancé and strangely from that moment she had begun to claw back her sanity and self-esteem. Hating him had helped, along with the bitter contempt she'd felt for a man who could be bought. The one small comfort she'd had was that she hadn't slept with Glen, however tempted she'd felt when their petting had got heated. She'd had a romantic vision of their wedding night being special. Special! Her lip curled as she sat down. But at least it had saved her from making the mistake of giving her virginity to that undeserving rat.

He'd married Julia the following May, and it had been a relief when, six months later, Glen's parents had moved to a small bungalow on the coast, their daughters now living in the centre of London in a student flat. Glen's parents hadn't liked Julia and had frequently reported she was making their son's life a misery, but Georgie hadn't wanted to know. The Glen chapter of her life was a closed book. But

it had left deep scars, how deep she hadn't fully acknowledged until she had come face to face with Matt de
Capistrano.

He was fabulously wealthy and arrogant and ruthless—
just like Julia Bloomsbury. He thought he only had to want
something for it to happen, that everything—people, values,
morals—could be bent to his will just because he could
buy and sell the average Mr Joe Bloggs a hundred times
over. Well, he was in for a surprise. Her green eyes flashed
like glittering emeralds and the last lingering sensation in-
duced by his kiss was burnt away.

People like Julia Bloomsbury and Matt had no conscience, no soul; they rode roughshod over people and
didn't even notice they were trampling them into the
ground. Money was their god, it bought them what they
wanted and that was all that mattered. And the meadow,
Newbottle Meadow, was a perfect example of that. She
hated him. Her chin rose and her shoulders straightened as
a little inner voice asked nastily why she was so adamant
about convincing herself of the fact.

'I do, I hate him.' She said it out loud, opening the
drawer of her desk and fishing out her wilting sandwiches
as she did so. 'And the sooner he accepts that the better
it'll be for both of us.'

And then she grimaced at the foolishness of talking to
herself, bit into her chicken and mayonnaise sandwich and
determined to put all further thoughts of Matt de Capistrano
out of her mind.

CHAPTER FOUR

AFTER eating her lunch Georgie was on the phone for more than an hour searching for a venue for the children's party. She drew a blank at all the community and church halls in the district, and the prices one or two of them wanted to charge were exorbitant anyway for someone in Robert's current position. She then decided Robert would have to allow her to hold the twins' party at home and he could disappear for the afternoon, after he had helped her set up, but trying to hire a bouncy castle for that particular day proved just as fruitless.

Eventually she put all thoughts of the party on hold and decided to type up the notes from the morning before attacking the rest of her workload.

She worked like a beaver all afternoon, clearing a vast mountain of paperwork and dealing with the men's wages when they called in later in the day. There was still no sign of Robert at four o'clock and then at ten past she heard the door open and looked up expectantly. 'Where have you been—?' She stopped abruptly. Instead of Robert's pleasant face Matt de Capistrano was looking at her, his eyes molten as they roved over her creamy skin and golden hair.

She tried to make a casual comment, to look away and busy herself with the papers on her desk, but she could not. She felt transfixed, hypnotised, and as her heart began to pound at the expression on the dark face she told herself to open her mouth, to say *anything*. 'I thought you were Robert,' she managed weakly.

'But as you see I am not,' he returned coolly.

'No...' Oh, what an inane conversation, she told herself angrily. Say something sensible, for goodness' sake! 'Do you know where he is?'

'We had a few hitches on site after lunch, potential drainage and so on, so we've been pretty tied up all afternoon,' Matt said quietly. 'He should be here in a few minutes; he was leaving just after me.'

She nodded in what she hoped was a brisk secretarial fashion. 'Your notes are all ready.' She wrenched her gaze from his and pointed at the large white envelope on one side of the desk. 'I hope I got everything down and—'

'You're incredibly lovely,' he said slowly. 'And without artifice. Most women of my acquaintance put on the war paint before they even get out of bed in the morning.'

And no doubt you speak from experience, she thought tartly. 'Really?' she managed a polite smile. 'Now, regarding the west part of the site, where the architect said—'

'Damn the architect.' He had moved to stand in front of her and now, as her surprised eyes met his, he said softly, 'Have dinner with me tonight?'

Was he mad? She stared at him, her cheeks flushing rosy pink as her eyes fell on to the V below his throat where his shirt buttons were undone to expose a tantalisingly small amount of tanned skin and the beginnings of dark body hair. She snapped her eyes upwards but it was too late; her body was already tingling. As much in answer to her own traitorous response to his maleness she said very stiffly, 'That is quite out of the question, as I thought I made perfectly clear this morning.'

'Would it help if I kissed you again?' he asked contemplatively.

Just you try it! You'll soon know what it feels like to have a word processor on top of your head. She glared at him and her face must have spoken for itself because he nodded thoughtfully. 'Perhaps not,' he acknowledged drily.

He was enjoying this! It was just a game to him, a diversion! 'I have plenty of work to do if you've quite finished,' she snapped angrily.

'Finished? I haven't even started.' And his smile was a crocodile smile.

'Wrong.' Georgie's gaze was sharp. 'I haven't got time to bandy words with you, Matt.'

'Then cut out the necessity and have dinner with me,' he responded immediately.

What did it take to get it into that thick skull of his that she would rather dine with Hannibal Lecter? 'No.' It was final. 'I like to get dinner while I listen to the children tell me about their day and then we all dine together. They need that sort of reassurance in their lives at the moment.'

'And you don't ever have an evening off?'

'No.'

'Then I will pick you up about nine, yes? Once they are in bed,' he drawled silkily, his accent very strong as he stared down at her, his hands thrust into the pockets of his jeans and a shaft of sunlight from the window turning his hair blue-black.

'For the last time, I am not going to have dinner with you!'

It was unfortunate that Robert chose that precise moment to walk into the building. Georgie saw him stop dead, his eyes flashing from her pink face to Matt's coolly undisturbed one, before he said, 'Problems?'

'Not at all,' Matt said easily. 'I asked Georgie to have dinner with me tonight but she informs me she feels the children need her at the moment and she has to stay at home.'

'Georgie, you don't have to do that—'

'I want to, Robert.' She cut off her brother's protest abruptly.

'Well if you're at a loose end tonight why don't you join *us* for dinner?' Robert asked Matt in the next moment, much to Georgie's horror. 'It's not exactly restful, so I warn you before you say yea or nay. The kids are always pretty hyper at the end of the day, but you're welcome.'

'Great, I'd love to.' It was immediate and Matt didn't look at Georgie.

'Good. Problem solved.' Robert smiled happily at them both and for the first time since Sandra's death Georgie felt the urge to kick him. It had happened fairly frequently through her growing up years, but never as strongly as now.

'But…' Matt turned to Georgie as he spoke and she just knew the tentative expression on his face wasn't genuine. 'Will there be enough for an extra mouth at such short notice?'

She would have loved to have said no, because she knew as well as he did that she had been manoeuvred into a corner, but she gritted her teeth for a second and then said brightly, 'If you like pot roast?'

'Love it.'

'Oh, good.'

And then she ducked her head to hide the acid resurgence of bitterness that had gripped her. Manipulating, cunning, Machiavellian, underhand—

'White wine or red?'

'What?'

Robert had walked through into his office but Matt had paused at the interconnecting doorway. 'I said, white wine or red?' he said easily, the gleam of amusement in the grey eyes telling Georgie all too clearly he had known exactly what she was thinking.

'Whatever,' she growled ungratefully.

'Right.' And then he had the audacity to add—purely for Robert's benefit, she was sure, 'It's been a long time since I've enjoyed a family evening round a pot roast; I really appreciate the kindness.'

Add hypocritical and two-faced to the other list, Georgie thought balefully as the door closed and she was alone, her teeth clamped together so hard they were aching.

Matt was only ensconced with Robert for some five minutes before he emerged again, stopping by her desk and picking up the envelope as he said, 'When and how do you want me?'

'What?' The ghastly sexual awareness that took her over whenever she was within six feet of this man made her voice breathless.

'Dinner?' He smiled innocently. 'What time and how do I dress? Formal or informal?'

Impossible man! She kept her voice very prim and proper as she said, 'Half-past six. I don't like the twins to eat too late as their bedtime is eight o'clock. And informal, very. The children might even be in their pyjamas if there's a programme on TV they want to watch after dinner and they've finished any homework they have.'

'Homework?' He wrinkled his aristocratic nose. 'Poor little things. Why are children not allowed to be children these days? There is enough time for the homework and other such restrictions when they are a little older.'

She agreed with him absolutely but she wasn't about to tell him that. 'They have to learn a certain amount of discipline,' she said evenly as her stomach churned at the thought of the forthcoming evening.

'How stern you sound.' His voice made it very clear he didn't rate her as an aunty and it rankled—unbearably. She hadn't been cast in the role of Wicked Witch of the West before. 'Half-past six it is, then. Robert's given me the address.'

Georgie waited until she was sure Matt's Lamborghini had left and then knocked on Robert's door before she popped her head round to say, 'There's a couple of things I need to get for dinner so I'll see you at home later, okay?'

'Georgie?' As she made to withdraw, Robert's voice called her back. 'You didn't mind me inviting him, did you? I didn't think at the time, but you're doing enough looking after me and the kids without me asking along any Tom, Dick or Harry.'

Matt de Capistrano was definitely not your average Tom, Dick or Harry, Georgie thought wryly, but as she looked into her brother's eyes—the lines of strain and grief all too evident on Robert's countenance—she said brightly, 'Of course not; it pays to keep him sweet at the moment, doesn't it? And the kids will like a guest for a change. Just don't make a habit of it, eh?'

'You're a brick, and take the car. I'll get a taxi later.'

A brick she might be, but this particular brick was going to have to vamp up a boring old pot roast into something great, and she only had a couple of hours to do that, clean the house, make the children presentable and a hundred and one other things that were *absolutely* imperative if Matt de Capistrano was going to set foot across the threshold of their home.

After buying two very extravagant desserts, flowers for the table, a packet of wildly expensive coffee and a good bottle of brandy, Georgie drove home at breakneck speed to find the children involved in building a castle of Lego with the middle-aged 'grandmother' from next door who came in to sit with them each day when they got home from school.

Five minutes later—with Mrs Jarvis happily toddling

home after her customary little chat—the house was a scene of feverish activity. Once the sitting room was cleared of every piece of Lego, Georgie organised David vaccing downstairs and Annie dusting, whilst she dressed up the pot roast with cream and wine and quickly prepared more vegetables and a pot of new potatoes to add to the roast potatoes she had peeled that morning.

That done, she marshalled the children upstairs to bath and change into their clean pyjamas, whilst she set the table in the dining room with the best crockery and cutlery and arranged the flowers she had bought earlier.

The children downstairs again, looking demure and sweet as they sat on the sofa in front of their favourite video, Georgie flew upstairs to shower and change after spraying the house with air freshener and lighting scented candles in the dining room.

She heard Robert arrive home as she stepped out of the shower, and shouted for him to check the vegetables before she dived into the bedroom she shared with Annie and pulled on a pair of casually smart trousers and a little fig-ure-hugging top in bubblegum-pink cashmere.

Too dressed up. She looked at herself in the mirror and gave a flustered groan. Definitely. The children would be sure to make some comment and then she would just die.

She whipped off the trousers and replaced them with a pair of old and well-washed jeans. Better. She stood for a moment contemplating her reflection. Yes, that was just the right note and this top *was* gorgeous; she couldn't consign it the same way as the trousers.

Her hair only took a minute or two to dry, courtesy of her hairdryer, falling in a soft silky veil about her face, and apart from her usual touch of mascara on her fair eyelashes she didn't bother with any make-up. She had just fixed her big silver hoops in her ears when she heard the doorbell ring, and her stomach turned right over.

'Calm, girl, calm.' She shut her eyes tightly before opening them and gazing into the mirror. 'This is nothing. You've had guests for dinner in the past, for goodness' sake, and that is all Matt de Capistrano is. Get it into perspective.'

The faltering perspective received a death blow when she walked into the sitting room a few moments later. The two men were standing with a glass of wine in their hands and Matt's hard profile was towards her as he listened to something Annie was telling him. He was giving the child his full attention and was not yet aware of her, but as Georgie looked at his impressively male body clothed in black trousers and an open-necked charcoal shirt her breath caught in her throat. *He was gorgeous.* It was the last thing she either needed or wanted to think. And dangerous. Infinitely dangerous.

And then he turned towards her and she was caught in the light of his eyes, and she had never felt so vulnerable or unprepared. 'Hallo, Matt.'

'Hallo, Georgie,' he murmured softly, her name a caress as his accent gave it a sensuality that made her innermost core vibrate.

'I'll...I'll just see to the dinner.' She fled into the kitchen and then stood for a moment or two just staring helplessly around her. What was she going to do? *What was she going to do?* And then the panic subsided as cold reason said, Nothing. You are going to do nothing but play the hostess. This is one night in a lifetime and once it is over you can have a quiet word with Robert and make sure he doesn't repeat the invitation. Simple.

By the time they all walked through to the dining room it was clear Annie was in love and David had a severe case of hero worship. Georgie had drunk two glasses of wine on an empty stomach, however, and her Dutch courage was high as she watched the children hang on Matt's every word.

'And you *really* have some horses in Spain and here as well?' Annie was asking as Georgie brought in the last of the dishes. Annie was horse-mad and had been having riding lessons for the last year. 'What are they like?'

'Beautiful.' Matt's eyes stroked over Georgie's face for the briefest of moments as he said the word, and then his gaze returned to the animated child. 'You could perhaps come and see them some time if your father wishes it?'

'Really?' It was said on a whoop of delight. 'You mean it?'

'I never say anything I do not mean.' And again Georgie felt the glittering gaze pass over her, although she was intent on removing the lids of the steaming dishes. 'Of course I mean the ones in England,' he added teasingly. 'Spain would be rather a long way to go to see a horse, would it not?'

'I wouldn't mind.' Annie's tone made it clear she would go to the end of the earth if Matt was there and Georgie gave a wry smile to herself. Any age and they'd go down before that dark charm like ninepins. He had a magnetism that was fascinating if you were foolish enough to forget the ruthless and cold mind behind it.

'That's very good of you, Matt.' It was obvious Robert was a little taken aback and not at all sure if this was a social pleasantry said lightly but without real intent.

And then Matt disabused him of that idea when he said, 'Why not this weekend, if you aren't doing anything? You and the children and Georgie could come for the day and have a look round the estate. It would be a distraction for the little ones.' This last was said in an undertone to Robert, and then Matt added to David, 'And bring your swimming trunks, yes? I have a pool and you can practise your breast stroke.'

So David had told him he and Annie were learning to swim at the local baths at some point when she had been busy in the kitchen? And Matt, being Matt, hadn't missed a trick. Horses and a pool—he really was the man who had everything. But not as far as she was concerned.

Georgie kept her voice light and pleasant as she said, 'Tuck in, everyone, and I'm sure the children would love a day out. Unfortunately I shan't be able to make it this weekend as I'm meeting an old university friend who is down in London for a few days, but you and the children must go, Robert.'

'Your friend is very welcome to come along too,' Matt said just as pleasantly.

'Thank you, but I think we'll leave it as it is.' Georgie offered him the dish of roast potatoes as she spoke and as their fingers touched she felt an electric shock shoot right down to her toes.

'Your friend doesn't like horses?' She'd seen the awareness in his eyes and knew the physical contact had registered on him too.

'I don't know.'

'You could ask her.'

Enough was enough. He could try his big-brother tactics on everyone else but she was not having any of it. 'Simon is the quiet type.' She saw the name connect in the dark eyes and assumed a smiling mask to cover up the apprehension his narrowed gaze was causing. 'He doesn't like crowds.'

'He would consider six a crowd?' The mocking voice carried an edge of steel which said only too plainly such a man would be an out-and-out wimp.

Georgie shrugged dismissively. She didn't trust herself to speak without telling him exactly what she thought of him, and that was not an option with the twins present; neither did she think it opportune to mention that Simon was engaged to be married to her best friend from her university days, and that he'd asked her to help in selecting a piece of jewellery to give to his bride as a surprise wedding present.

'I'm going to be eight soon.' Annie cut into the awkward moment and Georgie could have kissed her niece. 'So is David 'cos we're twins.'

'Right.' Matt nodded as he smiled into the little girl's openly admiring face.

'I think I should have been eight ages ago,' Annie continued firmly. 'Stuart Miller is nearly nine and he can't spell yet. Can he, David?'

David had his mouth full of pot roast and merely shook his head in agreement.

'And me and David know really big words.' Annie's massive blue eyes were fixed on the object of her adoration. 'Have you got any children at home?'

Georgie choked on a piece of potato. Never let it be said that Annie was backward in coming forward! However, by the end of the meal Georgie had discovered plenty about Matt de Capistrano through Annie's innocent chattering. He was the product of an English mother and Spanish father and had one sibling, a sister, who had produced a quiverful of children. His father had died several years ago and his mother continued to reside in her own home in Spain, where Matt also had business interests. He had homes in both countries and divided his time equally between them, and he liked horses and dogs and cats. This last was important to Annie, who had decided she wanted to be a vet when she grew up. And his favourite colour was green.

This last question was answered along with a glance at Georgie and the grey eyes smiled mockingly.

Oh, yes, she just bet, Georgie thought silently as she returned the smile politely without giving anything away. And with a blue-eyed blonde it would be blue, and a brown-eyed brunette brown and so on.

Once dinner was over Georgie shooed everyone into the sitting room and retired to the sanctuary of the kitchen, refusing any offers of help, where she dallied until the children's bedtime. She spent longer than normal upstairs with them and then when they were both asleep and it became impossible to delay the moment a second longer, she made her way downstairs, glancing at her watch as she did so. Half-past nine. In another half an hour or so, once she had made them all more coffee, she could gracefully retire and leave the two men to talk. This evening might not be as bad as she had feared.

She realised her mistake as soon as she entered the sitting room. 'Georgie, did you find anywhere to have the kids' party?' Robert asked before she had even shut the door behind her.

'The party?' She was desperately aware of the dark figure sitting to one side of the open French windows on the perimeter of her vision but she kept her eyes on Robert. 'No, no, I didn't, as it happens. I'll try again tomorrow and—'

'Don't worry, Matt's had the most brilliant idea,' Robert interrupted her.

'He has?' She darted one quick wary glance Matt's way and saw the dark face was totally expressionless. It was not reassuring.

'As you can't make this weekend he's offered for us all to go over the next and have the kids' party at his place.'

Robert imparted this news as though it wasn't the most horrendous thing he could have said.

For a moment Georgie was too astounded to say anything, but then reason came back in a hot flood. 'We couldn't possibly,' she protested quickly. 'It's very kind, of course, but they will want their schoolfriends to their party. It's far better we leave things as they are.'

'I meant for their friends to be invited.' Matt was sitting on the large oak chest used to store the children's huge collection of Lego and now he folded his arms over his chest, settling more comfortably on the wood as he surveyed her flushed face with an air of cool determination. 'I bought an old farm some time ago and had the place gutted and rebuilt, and there's plenty of land for the children to enjoy themselves in. The pool is indoors and heated, so they can let off some steam in there, and we can have that bouncy castle on the lawn outside the house if it's fine or in one of the old barns if the weather is inclement. And all kids love a barbecue.'

'I…I couldn't get a bouncy castle,' Georgie said weakly. 'There's not one for hire.'

'There will be if I want one,' Matt said smoothly. 'I've suggested to Robert you have a run over to my place now so you can satisfy yourself it would be okay; it's only half-an-hour's drive.'

This was going from bad to worse. 'I don't think—'

'We can make a day of it,' Matt continued evenly, 'and any parents who want to stay for the day are welcome, or if they just want to come back for the barbecue in the evening that's fine too. My staff are used to large social gatherings and there's a very good catering firm my house-keeper uses at such times.'

His *staff*?

'So it could be a morning by the pool and a buffet lunch,

followed by the bouncy castle and a magician and so on in the afternoon with an evening barbecue,' he continued seamlessly.

'Matt—'

'Do you think David and Annie would enjoy that?' he added with innocent deadly intent. It was the clincher and they both knew it.

How could she deprive David and Annie of such a treat? Georgie asked herself silently. She couldn't. And this master strategist had played her like a virtuoso playing a violin. But he was mad; he had to be. To do all this just because she had refused to have a date with him? This was megalomania at its worst.

'That's settled, then.' Robert appeared to be quite unaware of the electric undercurrents in the room as he nodded from one to the other of them. 'I'll get the coffee on, Georgie. You sit down for a while; you've not stopped all day.'

Before she could stop him Robert had bustled out of the room. Georgie, still coping with her shock, sank down on to the sofa before she realised she should have chosen the single safety of a chair, and the fact was emphasised when Matt sat down beside her in the next moment, slanting a look at her from under half-closed lids.

'I'd genuinely like to give the twins a treat after what they have been through, Georgie,' he said quietly. 'They're nice children, both of them.'

His thigh was touching hers and she had never been so aware of another human being's body in her life, and it took a moment or two before she could say, forcing sarcasm into her voice, 'And that's why you offered to accommodate hordes of screaming infants for the day? Pure magnanimity?'

'Ah, now that's a different question.' He shifted slightly

on the sofa and her senses went into overdrive. He was half turned towards her, one arm along the back of the sofa behind her, and she felt positively enclosed by his dark aura, enclosed and held. 'I've never pretended to be "pure" anything.'

He was doing it again. Laughing at her in that dark smoky voice of his, although there was no trace of amusement on the hard male face. She had made the mistake of raising her eyes to his and now she found it impossible to look away.

'Will you come with me tonight?' The words themselves were nothing, but the way he said them sent a shiver of something hot and sensual down her spine.

'I...I can't.' She gestured helplessly towards the dusky twilight outside the window. 'It's dark now, and late. And...and Robert's getting the coffee.' There was no way—*no way*—she was leaving here with Matt de Capistrano tonight, not with him looking and smelling like the best thing since sliced bread, Georgie thought feverishly. She needed time to distance herself again, get her emotions under control and let cold reason take the place of sexual attraction. But how long—the nasty little voice that was forever making itself known these days asked— how long would that take? An hour? A day? A month?

'Okay.' His voice was soft, silky soft. 'It's probably better you see it in the light anyway. Tomorrow, then. I will call in the office and drive you out there before you come home.'

'I don't need to see your home, Matt, I'm sure it's fine,' she had the presence of mind to say fairly firmly.

'I insist.' It was firmer still.

'But—'

'And then if there is anything you are not happy with— matters of safety, that sort of thing—we can sort it before the party. You'll be quite safe,' he added mockingly as he lifted her small chin and gazed down into the sea-green eyes with a cynical smile. 'My housekeeper and her husband, who oversees the gardens for me, live in, and my groom has his own purpose-built flat above the stables so there are always people about.'

His thick black lashes turned his eyes into bottomless pools, Georgie thought weakly. And then she took a hold of herself, straightening slightly as she removed her chin from his fingers with a flick of her head. 'I didn't think my safety was in question,' she said stiffly, and then was mortified when he laughed softly.

'Little liar.'

His smoky amusement made her face flame. 'No, really—'

'You were worried I would do this...' He put his mouth to hers and stroked her sealed lips lightly, the scent of him heady in her nostrils. He wasn't touching her now except by their joined mouths, but he might as well have been because Georgie was utterly unable to move.

The kiss was sweet, even chaste for a few moments, and then the hand on the back of the sofa slipped down into the small of her back and she found herself drawn into the hard steel of his body as her lips opened beneath his. And he was ready for her, plunging swiftly into the secret contours of her mouth as his tongue and his lips created such a wild rush of sensation she moaned softly, trembling slightly.

His other hand was lightly cupping one breast now through the baby-soft wool, and as he began a slow erotic rhythm on the hardening peak that caused little tremors of passion to shiver in ever-increasing waves Georgie felt drugged with passion.

He was good. He was so good at this. The acknowledgement of his expertise was on the edge of her consciousness and didn't affect the tumultuous emotions which had taken hold.

She could feel the solid pounding of his heart under the thin charcoal silk and as he pulled her even closer his body told her he was as aroused as she was. And it felt so good, *wonderful* to know she could affect him in this way, Georgie admitted fiercely.

Her hands had been curled against the solid wall of his muscled chest, but now they moved up to the powerful shoulders as she moaned softly in her throat and he answered the unspoken need with a guttural sound of his own.

He had turned her into the soft back of the sofa at some point as his body covered hers, and now, as the trembling in her body was reflected in his, he raised his head, his eyes glittering in the semi-light of the standard lamp Robert had switched on earlier. 'You see?' he murmured softly. 'You want me as much as I want you, Georgie. The chemistry is red-hot.'

She was breathing hard now his lips had left hers, and although part of her was crying out in mute protest at the declaration, she was having to fight the urge to reach up for his mouth again. And she mustn't, she mustn't. He had already stormed her defences and caused an abandonment that was only fully dawning on her now his mouth had left hers.

She stared at him, her eyes huge. 'This…this is just sex,' she whispered shakily.

'I know.' He smiled, a sexy quirk of his firm mouth. 'Great, is it not?'

'It isn't enough, not for me.' She pushed at him and he immediately released her, his hand returning to the back of the sofa as he still continued to lean over her without touching her now. His retreat gave her the courage to say more firmly, 'I mean it, Matt. I don't want this.' She drew in a deep breath and added, 'All I want is for you to leave me alone. That's not too much to ask, is it?'

'Much too much,' he said with quiet finality. 'I have tasted you twice now and I want more, much more. But I can be patient, believe it or not.'

'All the patience in the world won't alter my mind.'

'And I never back down from a challenge,' he warned softly.

So she had been right; he saw her as a challenge because she hadn't immediately fallen gratefully into his arms, Georgie thought hotly, her anger banishing the last remnants of his lovemaking and putting iron in her limbs. 'I have absolutely no intention of having a relationship with you,' she stated very coldly, 'or anyone else for that matter. Robert and the twins are my prime concern at the moment, but even if they weren't around I wouldn't sleep with you. Is that clear enough?'

'Abundantly.'

At least he wasn't smiling now, she thought a trifle hysterically, before she said, 'Good. I'm glad you've seen sense at last.'

He muttered something dark and Spanish and—Georgie was certain—uncomplimentary under his breath, and had just opened his mouth to reply when Robert called from outside the door, 'Georgie? Open the door, would you? I've a tray in my hands,' and she leapt up and fairly flew across the room.

It was another twenty minutes before Matt stood up to leave and Georgie was amazed at his acting ability. If it wasn't for the steely glint in his eyes when he glanced her way she might have been convinced she had imagined the whole episode from the way he was smiling and conversing with Robert.

'That was a wonderful dinner, Georgie.' As the three of them stood on the doorstep his voice was the epitome of a satisfied guest thanking his hostess. 'You certainly know the way to a man's heart,' he added smoothly.

Sarcastic so-and-so! Georgie smiled sweetly. 'So it has been said,' she agreed demurely.

She saw the grey eyes spark and then narrow, and reminded herself to go carefully. Matt de Capistrano was not a man it was wise to annoy, but he made her so *mad*.

The telephone had started to ring in the sitting room. Robert said, 'I'm sorry, Matt, do you mind if I get that?'

Matt was already shaking his head and saying, 'No, you go and I'll see you tomorrow.'

'Goodnight, Matt.'

The two of them were alone now, and in answer to her dismissive voice he smiled. 'Walk me to my car.'

She didn't have time to agree or disagree before he took her arm and whisked her down the shadowed drive.

'Let go of me!' Her voice was on the edge of hostility but she was desperately trying to remain calm; Matt *was* Robert's bread and butter, after all.

'I like you better when you are soft and breathless in my arms than spitting rocks,' he drawled with mocking composure.

Her face bloomed with colour and Georgie was desperately glad of the scented darkness which hid her blushes as she breathed, 'I *told* you to forget all that.'

'Have there been many?' he asked with sudden seriousness, his hand still on her arm.

'What?' She stared at him, bewildered by the abrupt change.

'Men who have complimented you on your dinners,' he said with silky innuendo.

'That's my business.' She was shocked and it showed. How *dared* he question her about her love life? Not that she had one at the moment, and the last three years hadn't been anything to write home about, either, if she was being honest. She had had the occasional date after Glen, of course, but after a time she had begun to wonder why she was bothering to make the effort when there wasn't anyone she remotely fancied. She knew she didn't want to get involved with anyone again—certainly not for a long, long time anyway, if at all—and even when she made it perfectly clear the date was on a purely friends basis, the man in question always had to try and paw her about at the end of the evening. And so she had made up her mind that unless that magical 'something' was there she was content to be single. And it hadn't been. Until now. She shuddered as the last two words hit.

'You're cold.' He enfolded her into his arms as he spoke, but loosely, his fingertips brushing her lower ribs and the palms of his hands cupping her sides. 'You should be wearing something more than that pink thing out here.'

The warm fragrance of him was all about her and the harnessed strength in the big male body caused a fluttering inside that Georgie recognised with a stab of disgust at her own weakness. 'I didn't plan to be out here, if you remember,' she said as tartly as she could, considering her legs were like jelly. 'And the "pink thing", as you call it, is a very expensive cashmere top that cost me an arm and a leg.'

'Which arm and which leg?' He drew her closer, so they were thigh to thigh and breast to breast. 'They all feel like the real thing.'

She tried to push away but it was like pushing against solid steel. 'Matt, please.'

'Yes, Georgie?' His eyes moved to the soft gold of her hair for a moment.

'I...I have to go in.' It wasn't as firm as she would have liked.

'Okay.' He didn't relax his hold an iota. 'But first you repeat after me: I will be ready and waiting when you arrive to pick me up tomorrow night, Matt.'

'But I told you I don't need to see your house; I'm sure it's quite suitable and—'

'No, that was not right. I will be ready and waiting when you arrive to pick me up tomorrow night, Matt,' he repeated softly, his dark body merging into the shadows like a creature of the night.

'Matt!' She wriggled but it was useless. 'Robert will see us.'

'Good.'

'I'll scream.'

Georgie looked at him steadily and saw he was vastly amused. Oh, this was ridiculous! What must they look like? But he wasn't going to give in; she could read it in the dark, aggressively attractive face looking down at her. Well, one quick visit to his house wouldn't hurt, would it? She could make it clear she had to be back in time to get the children's dinner and so on, she comforted herself silently. 'I will be ready and waiting when you arrive to pick me up tomorrow night, Matt.'

'That wasn't so bad, was it?' Grey eyes softened to warm charcoal. 'I'll be at the office for five, yes?'

'And I must be home to get the twins' tea.'

'Cinderella, twenty-first century,' he murmured softly. 'But first you shall go to the ball.' And he kissed her, long and hard until she was breathless, and then put her aside and slid into the Lamborghini seemingly in one fluid movement.

She was still standing exactly as he had placed her, one hand touching her tingling bruised lips, when he roared out of the drive into the street in a flash of gleaming metal. And then he was gone.

CHAPTER FIVE

GEORGIE didn't sleep much that night. She spent most of the long silent hours trying to sort out her feelings, but by the time a pale, pink-edged dawn crept stealthily over the morning sky she'd given it up as hopeless. This was disturbing and outside her understanding, or more to the point Matt de Capistrano was disturbing and outside her understanding! She corrected herself wryly. And she didn't want to feel like this; it horrified her.

For the last few years she had been in control. Once she had recovered from the caustic fall-out of Glen's rejection she had changed her mindset and her goals. She had known exactly what she was doing, where she was going and what she was aiming for. And now...now she wasn't sure about anything and it terrified her; in fact it was totally unacceptable.

For some reason Matt's dark face seemed to be printed on the screen of her mind. She didn't want it there, in fact she would give anything to have it wiped clean, but somehow there it stayed.

She was sitting in front of the bedroom window, Annie asleep in her small single bed in one corner of the room, and as the small child stirred and then settled down to sleep again Georgie's eyes remained on her. It was true what she had said to Matt, she told herself fiercely. She had more than enough to do to cope with the twins and Robert. If he couldn't understand that then it was tough.

She turned and looked outside again to where an adolescent song thrush was sitting in the copper beech outside the bedroom window. Its bright black eyes surveyed her for one moment and it seemed to hesitate before rising up into the sky in a glorious swoop of freedom, the earth and all its dangers and difficulties forgotten in the wonder of being alive. She mustn't hesitate either. She nodded to the thought as though it had been spoken out loud. Matt had made it quite clear he wanted her for one thing and one thing only, and if she didn't put him behind her and escape—like that bird into the sky—he would clip her wings in a way Glen would never have been able to do. She had recovered from Glen; she had a feeling Matt de Capistrano was the sort of man you never recovered from.

At five o'clock she was in the shower and by six she was dressed and downstairs, preparing breakfast for everyone and four packed lunches. She paused in the middle of spreading mashed egg and salad cream on to buttered bread, glancing round the small homely kitchen as she did so. What had Matt thought of this home? His lifestyle was so different as to be another world away. He had staff to cater to his wants, to serve him breakfast and anticipate his every need. And in his love life she was sure there were plenty of willing women to supply everything he needed there too! He was rich, ruthless, selfish and shallow. *He was*. She reiterated it in her mind and didn't question why she needed to convince herself of his failings. She saw it clearly now, she reassured herself as the pile of sandwiches grew. Crystal-clear.

The crystalline certainty continued until the moment she saw Matt.

He arrived prompt at five and drove her away from the office after a word or two with Robert in private, and when the Lamborghini entered a winding drive some twenty-five

minutes later, after a sign which said, 'Private. El Dorado'.
She turned to him with questioning eyes.

'It means the golden land,' he answered her softly, 'a
country full of gold and gems.'

'And have you filled your El Dorado with gems?' she
asked a little cynically. No doubt the house would be a
monument to his success and full of all the trappings of
wealth. Which was fine, of course it was, if that was what
he wanted. It fitted the image.

'In a manner of speaking,' he answered somewhat cryp-
tically.

She opened her mouth to ask him what he meant, but
the words hovering on her tongue were never voiced as in
that same moment the car turned a corner in the drive and
the sort of sprawling thatched farmhouse that belonged in
fairy stories came into view.

'Oh, wow...' It wasn't particularly articulate but the look
on her enchanted face must have satisfied Matt because he
smiled slowly after bringing the car to a halt on the end of
the horseshoe-shaped drive.

'Come and have a look round inside first,' he suggested
quietly, 'and then I'll show you where we could have the
barbecue if it is wet, and of course the bouncy castle.'

His accent lent a quaintness to the last two words that
made her heart twang slightly, and as they walked up the
massive stone steps towards the big oak door she said, aiming to keep the conversation practical and mundane, 'This
is very nice; did you have to do much work to get it to this
point?'

'The place was almost derelict when I purchased it,' he
said, taking her arm as he opened the front door to reveal
a large hall panelled in mellow oak that was golden in the
sunlight slanting in from several narrow windows above
them. 'An old lady, the unmarried daughter of the original

farmer, had lived here for years alone, getting more and more into debt as the house fell down about her ears.'

'What a shame.' As Matt closed the front door Georgie stared at the curving staircase a few yards away which was a beautiful thing all on its own. 'Why did she decide to sell in the end?'

'She became too arthritic to continue,' he said shortly.

'Poor thing,' Georgie sympathised absently, her eyes on a fine painting on the far wall. 'She must have hated leaving her home.'

'Not so much the house, more the animals she had here,' Matt said quietly. 'She needed to go into a nursing home for proper care, but she had used the house and the grounds almost as a sanctuary for the remainder of her father's farm animals and the pets she had accumulated, who had grown old with her.'

Something in his voice caused her eyes to focus on him. If the person speaking had been other than Matt de Capistrano, ruthless tycoon and entrepreneur extraordinaire, she would have sworn there was tenderness colouring his words when he'd spoken of the old lady.

'What happened to them? To the animals?' Georgie asked softly.

Now his voice was expressionless, brisk even, when he said, 'You can meet a few, if you wish.' He had been leading her down the sun-kissed hall, which had bowls of fresh flowers on several occasional tables, and as they reached the far end he opened another door which led on to a large, white-washed passageway.

The opening of this last door caused a bell to tinkle somewhere, and in the next moment a big—very big—red-cheeked woman appeared from a doorway at the end of the passage, several dogs spilling out in front of her with a medley of barks and woofs.

'You kept them?' Georgie stopped abruptly and stared into his dead-pan face before she bent to fuss the excited animals who were now jumping round their feet. 'You kept the old lady's pets?'

'Aye, that he did, lass.' The woman—Matt's housekeeper, Georgie assumed—had now reached them and began shooing the dogs back into the room they had come from, continuing to say as she did so, 'We've more geriatrics here than in the nursing home where poor Miss Barnes is, bless her.' And then she straightened, holding out her hand as she said, 'I'm Rosie, by the way, Mr de Capistrano's housekeeper, and I'm very pleased to meet you, lass.'

She must have replied in like because everything continued quite normally for the next few minutes, but as Matt led her after Rosie, who had walked back into the massive farmhouse kitchen at the back of the house, Georgie's head was spinning. She was conscious of an overwhelming desire to take to her heels and run. This was danger—this place, the man at the side of her, all of it. He wouldn't stay in the niche she had made for him in her mind and it was imperative he did so.

This feeling continued as, after a tour of the farmhouse, which Matt had turned into a fabulous place, he took her outside into the surrounding grounds.

She had met what Rosie called 'the inside pests'—five dogs and several assorted cats—but now in the fields directly behind the house and to one side of the stable block she saw there was a small flock of ten or so sheep, two donkeys and several ancient horses meandering around along with one or two bony bovines.

'They took all her savings, most of her furniture and certainly her health,' Matt said quietly at the side of her as Georgie looked across at the animals pottering about in the sunshine. 'But she loved them more passionately than most people love their children. What could I do but agree they could live out their time quietly and peacefully here?'

'I suppose to her they *were* her children.' Georgie kept her voice even and steady although inside she felt as though she were drowning.

'Come and see my other gems,' Matt said lightly, seemingly unaware of the body blow he had wrought her. 'These are the 24-carat kind.'

She followed him into the stable block, where Matt's groom was working, and the young man joined them as Matt introduced her to his two thoroughbred Arab stallions and a dappled mare and young colt.

Okay, so he was kind to old ladies and animals, Georgie told herself silently as she listened to the two men talk about the merits of a new feed on the market. But she was neither, and she forgot that at her peril. He had already made it quite clear how he viewed an affair with her. It was a thing of the body, not of the mind, and the sexual attraction he felt for her would eventually burn itself out. And in view of her inexpertise in the bed department that might be a darn sight quicker than he had bargained for!

She was not a *femme fatale*, like his secretary or the women he normally associated with socially, and his world was as alien to her as—she searched her mind for an appropriate simile—as fish and chips out of a paper bag would be to him!

She ran her fingers over the raw silk coat of one of the stallions. The advertisement for a replacement secretary for Robert should be appearing in the paper tomorrow; hopefully she would soon be out of Matt's sphere and it wouldn't take long for a man like him to forget her.

'Magnificent, isn't he?' The warmth in Matt's voice brought her eyes from the horse to his face, and he turned to glance at her in the same moment. 'Do you ride?' he asked quietly.

'No.' There hadn't been any spare cash for anything so frivolous as riding lessons when she had been younger, and even now she knew Robert was struggling to pay for Annie's lessons.

'Would you like to?'

She shrugged, turning away from the stable and the horse's velvet nose which was twitching enquiringly over the half door. 'Annie's the horsewoman,' she said lightly. 'She'll go ape over this place.'

'Ape?'

'She'll love it,' Georgie explained as Matt fell into step beside her. 'She's crazy about animals although Robert and Sandra never wanted any. Your menagerie will be heaven on earth to her.'

'So I will be a means of satisfaction to at least one Millett female?' he enquired with silky mockery.

She ignored that, turning at the entrance into the stable block and waving to the young groom as she called her goodbyes.

Once outside in the mild May air she glanced about her as she said, 'You were going to show me where we could have the barbecue and bouncy castle if it is wet?'

'So I was. Please come this way, ma'am.' He imitated her brisk, no-nonsense voice with dark amusement and Georgie wanted to kick him, hard.

From the outside the large building some fifty yards to the left of the farmhouse looked like a big barn—but as Matt opened the huge wooden doors and they stepped inside Georgie saw it had been converted into what was basically a massive hall. A row of windows ran right round three walls at first-floor level and there was a stage at the far end where she presumed a band could play. To the side of the stage was a well-equipped bar, and a host of tables with chairs piled on them stood all along the right wall.

'Would this do?' Matt asked with suspicious meekness.

She nodded stiffly, suddenly vitally aware of the height and breadth of him beside her. 'It's very nice,' she said flatly.

'And the pool met your requirements?'

The pool had been terrific, more in keeping with a leisure centre than a private home, and being joined to the main house by means of a covered way off the well-equipped games room at the back of the house it was just as consumer-friendly in the winter as the summer. 'Everything's lovely,' she said reluctantly.

'Why don't we have a dip before dinner?' he suggested softly.

'I haven't got a swimming cos—' She stopped abruptly. 'Before *dinner*?'

He shut his eyes briefly at the shrill note and said patiently, 'People do, Georgie; it is quite a civilised way to live. I have a changing room full of suitable swimwear.'

And he knew exactly where he could stick it! She glared at him, berating herself for being so foolish as to trust him. 'You promised me you would take me straight home,' she said frostily. 'I need to look after the twins.'

'No, you do not,' he stated evenly. 'Robert might be just a mere man but he is more than able to take them out for a burger and then tuck them up in bed later. He is their father when all is said and done. Besides which...'

He hesitated, and Georgie eyed him with blazing green eyes as she clipped, 'Yes?'

'They need to bond, the three of them, and you are in danger of getting in the way,' he stated with unforgivable clarity.

'What?' Georgie couldn't believe her ears.

'You're pushing Robert out and swamping the twins with an over-indulgence of love in the process,' Matt stated quietly. 'Before long you'll have two brats on your hands if you aren't careful.'

Nothing in the world could have stopped her hand connecting with the hard tanned skin of his face. The slap echoed round the barn for some moments as they both stood stock still, looking at each other, Matt with a face of stone and Georgie wide-eyed and shaking. 'How dare you, how *dare* you say that when you have only met David and Annie once?' Georgie said painfully, her face reflecting her shock and hurt. 'They are wonderful kids, the pair of them.'

'I know that; I'm talking about what could happen in the future,' he grated tightly.

She called him a name that made his eyes widen and which surprised the pair of them. 'I want to go home right now,' she bit out furiously, her anger masking the horror that was now dawning as she saw her red handprint etched on the skin of his face.

'No way.' His eyes narrowed and she knew he meant it. 'You are going to stay here and have dinner with me whether you like it or not, and if you'd just take a little time to think about what I have said you might see there is some truth in it.'

'So you're saying I'm ruining the twins and stopping my brother from seeing his children?' Georgie asked wildly.

'*I am saying*—' He paused, moderating his tone before he continued more quietly, 'I am saying you need to let the three of them have some time together now and again, that is all. When was the last time Robert took David to the swimming baths or Annie to her riding lesson? When does he put them to bed and listen to what has happened in their day? When, Georgie?'

She stared at him, stunned and silent.

'David needs his father to go and see him when he has a football match now and again.' The dark husky voice was relentless. 'It is necessary and healthy.'

'Robert has had enough to do to cope with Sandra's death,' Georgie said fiercely.

'Initially, yes.' He allowed another brief pause before he said, 'But it has been six months, Georgie, and that is a long time in the life of a child. Robert has slipped into the habit of letting you be mother *and* father to the twins and I feel his wife, Sandra, would not have wanted this.'

'You didn't know her!'

'This is true.' The grey eyes were fixed on her stricken face. 'And this is why I can speak with impartiality. Sometimes it takes an outsider to see what is happening, and I do not doubt your love for your brother and his children but you cannot be their mother, Georgie. You are their aunty—precious, no doubt. But you will burn yourself out if you continue to try to be everything to everyone.'

Where had the shallow philanderer gone? She couldn't see him in this man who spoke with quiet but determined force and it scared her to death. And it was in challenge to that thought that she flung out, her voice scathing, 'All this talk about Robert and the twins when you know full well what you really want! You don't care about them; you're using them to get your own way. You are just the same as all the others!'

He was angry. Really, really angry. A muscle had knotted in his cheek and his grey eyes were steely, but his voice was even and controlled when he said, 'I'll ignore that because it is not worthy of a reply. You are a young woman of twenty-three and yet you act like a matron several decades older. When do you ever go out and enjoy yourself, Georgie? Have fun? Let your hair down?'

'With men, you mean?' she bit out with open hostility.

'We don't all need to sleep around to think we're having a good time. I like my life, as it happens.'

'I have it on good authority you have barely left the house in six months except to escort the children to and fro and go to work,' Matt returned harshly. 'That is not a life; that is an existence. Even this Simon is not what you led me to believe.'

'Excuse me?' He could only have got all this from Robert and she couldn't believe her brother had betrayed her in this way. Only it wouldn't have been like that, she reasoned in the next milli-second. Matt knew just how to word a question to get the maximum response and Robert would have been quite unaware he was being pumped for information. 'I did not "lead" you to believe anything!' she protested with outraged dignity.

'That is a matter of opinion.' He stared into her furious face, his own as angry, and then after a moment she saw him take a deep breath and visibly relax as he raked back his hair in a gesture that carried both irritation and frustration in it. 'Damn it, I did not want it to be like this,' he growled tightly.

She could believe that! Oh, yes, she could believe that all right. She knew quite well what he had had in mind. He had made sure of that himself—no strings attached and no heavy commitment was how he had termed it. He didn't believe in love or for everness. Well, if she was absolutely truthful, she wasn't quite sure what she believed in, but one thing she did know—when she made love with a man it would have to be believing there was at least a strong chance they would have some sort of a future together. It was just the way she was made and she wasn't going to apologise for that or anything else about herself either.

She drew herself up to her full five foot four inches and glared at him before turning out of the barn, but she had only gone a few steps when he caught at her arm, turning her round to face him. 'Would it help if I said if I was the twins' age you would be my ideal as a surrogate mother?' he asked with exaggerated humbleness.

'No,' she snapped hotly.

'Or that I think Robert is the luckiest brother in the world and that you have steered the good ship Millett through turbulent waters wonderfully well?'

'No again.'

In truth she was having a job not to cry, but she would rather die than let him know that. Maybe she *had* been a touch obsessional in trying to be everything the twins needed, but she could still remember how she had felt at ten years old when she had lost her parents and her world had disintegrated about her. But…but it *was* different for David and Annie. Her innate honesty was forcing the recognition in spite of herself. They still had their father, for a start, along with each other and the security of their home and all their friends. She had been whipped out of the environment she'd always known and placed with Robert and Sandra, and although they'd been wonderful, *marvellous*, it had been a terribly tough time. She *had* been overcompensating without realising it and in the process encouraging Robert to sit and brood rather than take his share of responsibility with the twins. *Oh, hell!*

'Georgie?' As she raised stricken eyes to Matt's face she saw he was watching her very closely. 'It is not criminal to have the kind heart,' he said softly. 'Better an excess of indulgence and pampering at this time than for them to feel cast adrift.'

If he had continued with the home truths in that cool relentless voice she could have coped, even the slightly mocking teasing attitude after he had caught her arm had kept the adrenaline running hot and strong, but this last was too much.

'I...I want to go home.' Her voice wobbled alarmingly over the declaration but she continued to fight the tears until the moment he pulled her into his arms, holding her against the solid warmth of his body. And then she just bawled her eyes out, in an unladylike display of wailing and choking sobs and a runny nose that was all out of proportion to anything which had gone before.

She couldn't have explained that her tears were as much for the lost little ten-year-old she had been as for Robert and Annie and David, for Glen's cruel cavalier treatment, for the humiliation and desperation she had felt at that time, and for Sandra. Poor, poor Sandra. Everything was all mixed up together and she cried as she hadn't done in years, not since her parents' death in fact.

Matt let her cry for long, long minutes, making no effort to ask any questions as he held her pressed against his chest and made soothing noises above her blonde head. And then, as the flood reduced to hiccuping sobs, and then valiant sniffs and splutters against his damp shirt-front, Georgie was overcome with embarrassment at her ignominious tears. How could she, how *could* she have lost control like that, and in front of Matt de Capistrano of all people? What must he be thinking? And then she found out.

'At a guess I would say that has been held in for far too long.' His voice was low and soft, his hands warm and soothing as they stroked her slender back. 'Am I right?'

Georgie stiffened slightly. This was a very astute and clever man in the normal run of things, and she had just given him a heaven-sent opportunity that even the thickest of individuals would capitalise on.

'I didn't mean to make you cry,' he continued quietly. 'You know that, don't you?'

'It wasn't you.' Her face was burning now, she could feel it, but she couldn't stay pressed against his chest for ever and so she pushed away from him, only to find he wasn't ready to let her go. She rubbed her pink nose, knowing she must look like something the cat had dragged in. 'Have you a hanky I can borrow?'

'In a moment.' He continued to look down into her tear-smudged face, into the startlingly green eyes that were so incredibly beautiful. 'If it was not my clumsy remarks, then what?'

'I...I don't know. Lots of things.' She heard her shaking voice with a dart of very real irritation at herself. She had to be strong and on her guard around Matt; trembling femininity was not an option. 'It's been a stressful time for everyone.'

'And you have been very brave.'

Oh, hell; if he kept this up she was going to blub all over him again, Georgie thought feverishly, as tears pricked at the back of her eyes again. After not crying for years it now seemed she couldn't stop!

'Not really.' She shrugged, trying to move out of his arms but not quite able to break free. 'I suppose the twins' situation is so close to the one I endured as a child that it makes it difficult to separate the two in my mind. The feelings I had then tend to get in the way sometimes.'

'Explain.' He let go of her long enough to delve into his pocket for a crisp white handkerchief, but after he had handed it to her and she was mopping at her face the strong arms enclosed her again, but lightly now, a few inches between them.

Not that it made much difference, Georgie thought a trifle hysterically. The big hard body, the delicious and literally intoxicating smell of him was all around her and it made her head spin. She had never in her wildest dreams believed that sexual attraction could be so strong or so physical, but it was making her legs weak.

She drew a deep breath, the handkerchief still clutched in one hand, and began to explain about the circumstances that had placed her in Robert's home.

He listened without interrupting until she had finished. 'So tiny and so ethereal.' There was what sounded like a note of disconcertment in the deep male voice. 'You appear at first sight to be...'

'The original dumb blonde?' she finished for him with a slight edge to her voice now, the memory of their first meeting suddenly very vivid. He had thought she was the type of female who spent all her time on the phone talking to other dumb females, then!

'Delicate and breakable,' he corrected evenly. 'But in truth you are—'

'As tough as old boots?' She did it on purpose, as much to annoy him and thereby shatter the intimate mood he'd created so effortlessly as to assure herself she was *not* going to be fooled by this new side of him.

'A very strong and courageous woman.' He tilted his head. 'You still haven't told me his name, Georgie.'

'Whose?' She had tried to hide the instinctive start she'd given at his ruthless strategy, but she knew the piercingly intent gaze had registered it.

'The man who has caused you to build this shell around yourself,' he said silkily.

He was not going to have this all his own way! She stared up at him, wondering why God had given him such a sexy mouth on top of all his other attributes, and said steadily, 'I could ask you the same question, Matt. You've told me you don't believe in love and for everness; there has to be a reason for that.'

He drew back and stared into her face, not able to hide

his surprise. And then his eyes narrowed and his hands fell from around her waist, and she knew she had hit a nerve. It was disturbing that it didn't give her the satisfaction she'd expected.

'Touché, Miss Millett.' His voice was cool, withdrawn, and in spite of herself she felt the loss of the warmth that had been there previously with a physical ache. 'So we are both...realistic; is that what you are saying?'

It wasn't at all what she had said and he knew it. She scrubbed at her face one last time and then offered him back the handkerchief. She could probe but, as she wasn't prepared to talk about Glen, it wouldn't be wise. She had said far too much already when she thought about it, all that about her childhood and so on. She wished now she had kept quiet.

'Come.' He held out his hand, his grey eyes unfathomable as he stared down into her heart-shaped face. 'I know just the thing to relax you and make you feel better,' he added with a touch of dark amusement.

Her imagination running rampant, Georgie peered up at him suspiciously. 'What's that?' she asked flatly.

'A swim, what else?' His smile was definitely of the wicked kind. 'As I said, I have many costumes in one of the changing rooms and you will find something suitable I am sure. We can swim a little, have a cocktail or two, and then change for dinner later.'

'I told you I'm not staying for dinner.'

'And I told you you are,' he said pleasantly. 'If nothing else, Rosie would be very upset to think you do not wish to partake of the meal she has been preparing most of the day.'

Georgie flushed. He was making her feel crass and it was so *unfair*. 'That's emotional blackmail,' she said tightly.

Matt shrugged and the gesture was very Latin. 'It is the truth.' And then his attitude changed somewhat as he added, 'I want to give you an evening off duty for once, Georgie; is that really such a crime? And Robert was in full agreement when I suggested this to him. "Very kind" was how he termed it, I think.'

Her flush deepened, and now the grey eyes were definitely laughing when he said, 'I promise to be a good boy at all times; does that help? I will treat you as I would treat my maiden aunt.'

He was standing in front of her, tall and lithe, his arms crossed over his broad chest and his shirt open at the bronze of his neck. He looked very masculine and dark and good enough to eat. Georgie swallowed hard. Impossible man. Impossible situation! 'All right.' She heard herself say the words with a faint feeling of despair. 'But just dinner, no swim.' Clothed, she could just about cope, but half-naked?

'You cannot swim?' he asked evenly. One dark eyebrow had slanted provocatively and she just *knew* he was sure of her answer.

'Yes.' It was reluctant.

'Then this is what we will do,' he stated firmly. 'Already Rosie will have taken the cocktails out to the pool area and I have had it heated warmer than usual so it will be quite pleasant. I have a swim before dinner each evening. It is very good for the circulation.'

Maybe, but the thought of Matt in next to nothing was playing havoc with her blood pressure.

And then he stretched out his hand again, this time taking one of hers as though he had a perfect right to touch her whenever he pleased, and she found herself walking alongside him as they made their way back to the house. She was all out of arguments.

GET FREE BOOKS and a FREE GIFT
WHEN YOU PLAY THE...

Just scratch off the silver box with a coin. Then check below to see the gifts you get!

SLOT MACHINE GAME!

YES! I have scratched off the silver box. Please send me the 2 free Harlequin Presents® books and gift for which I qualify. I understand I am under no obligation to purchase any books, as explained on the back of this card.

306 HDL DFTC

106 HDL DFTA
(H-P-OS-11/01)

NAME   (PLEASE PRINT CLEARLY)

ADDRESS

APT.#   CITY

STATE/PROV.   ZIP/POSTAL CODE

7	7	7	Worth TWO FREE BOOKS plus a BONUS Mystery Gift!
🍒	🍒	🍒	Worth TWO FREE BOOKS!
♣	♣	♣	Worth ONE FREE BOOK!
🔔	🔔	🍒	TRY AGAIN!

Visit us online at www.eHarlequin.com

DETACH AND MAIL CARD TODAY!

The Harlequin Reader Service® — Here's how it works:

Accepting your 2 free books and gift places you under no obligation to buy anything. You may keep the books and gift and return the shipping statement marked "cancel." If you do not cancel, about a month later we'll send you 6 additional novels and bill you just $3.34 each in the U.S., or $3.74 each in Canada, plus 25¢ shipping & handling per book and applicable taxes if any.* That's the complete price and — compared to cover prices of $3.99 each in the U.S. and $4.50 each in Canada — it's quite a bargain! You may cancel at any time, but if you choose to continue, every month we'll send you 6 more books, which you may either purchase at the discount price or return to us and cancel your subscription.

*Terms and prices subject to change without notice. Sales tax applicable in N.Y. Canadian residents will be charged applicable provincial taxes and GST.

If offer card is missing write to: Harlequin Reader Service, 3010 Walden Ave., P.O. Box 1867, Buffalo NY 14240-1867

BUSINESS REPLY MAIL
FIRST-CLASS MAIL   PERMIT NO. 717-003   BUFFALO, NY

POSTAGE WILL BE PAID BY ADDRESSEE

HARLEQUIN READER SERVICE
3010 WALDEN AVE
PO BOX 1867
BUFFALO NY 14240-9952

NO POSTAGE
NECESSARY
IF MAILED
IN THE
UNITED STATES

CHAPTER SIX

AN HOUR later, as Georgie lay on a thickly cushioned lounger at the side of the pool sipping an exotic pink cocktail, she had to admit to herself she was having a whale of a time.

Admittedly there had been several sticky moments. Firstly, when she had stood in the changing room used by Matt's female guests and looked at the vast row of minuscule bikinis and wraps, she had panicked big time. The tiny scraps of material all bore designer labels, and all seemed indecent to her fevered gaze, but eventually she had managed to find a one-piece among all the wisps which, although cut away at the sides and with a frighteningly plunging neckline, was a size eight and a little more decorous than the rest.

She had ignored the dozen or so diaphanous wraps, all gossamer-thin and quite beautiful in a rainbow of different colours, and regretfully reached for one of the towelling robes, which she had slipped on over the swimming costume and tied tightly round her waist.

She had glanced into the huge mirror which took up all of one wall at her reflection. The only thing showing were her feet and hands! She'd cope with the moment when she must find the nerve to disrobe later; this concealed almost every inch of her, and it had given her the courage to leave her hidey-hole with her head held high and her back straight.

Her cucumber-cool resolve had faltered somewhat when she'd emerged to find Matt climbing out of the pool, obviously having swum a few lengths while he was waiting for her.

He was wearing a pair of brief black swimming trunks which left nothing—absolutely nothing—to the imagination, and his thickly muscled torso had gleamed like oiled silk, the body hair on his chest a mass of tight black curls. She had known he would be magnificent unclothed, but the reality of the powerful male body, which didn't carry a morsel of fat and was primed to lean perfection, had been something else. Something dangerous and threatening and utterly mind-blowing.

She had forced herself to pad across towards him as he'd raised a casual hand in welcome, her mouth dry and the palms of her hands damp, but thankfully he had bent to pour out their drinks at her approach, and by the time she'd reached him she had pulled herself together.

'To the most beautiful maiden aunt anyone could wish to have,' he drawled mockingly as he placed one glass in her hand, raising his in a salute. 'And to a pleasant evening getting to know each other a little better.'

Georgie found it almost impossible to concentrate on anything else but the acres of hard tanned flesh in front of her, but somehow she found the strength to say, in a voice that could have passed for normal, 'To a nice evening,' as she raised her glass too. 'Mmm, that's gorgeous.' The cocktail tasted wonderful. 'What's in it?'

'Sloe gin, banana liqueur, crushed raspberries, white wine…and a couple of other things which are my secret,' Matt returned softly. 'I invented this cocktail a few years ago and there's many who would love to know the ingredients.'

'What's it called?' She took another gulp, needing something to distract her from the flagrant maleness in front of her, the taut belly and hard male thighs.

'Passionate Beginnings.' He was totally straight-faced.

She eyed him severely. 'You just made that up,' she accused uncertainly.

'Would I?' His voice was even softer now, and she shivered in spite of the hothouse warmth.

'You're not cold?' he asked in surprise.

'No, not cold exactly.' Her oxygen supply was in severe danger of running out and she felt weak at the knees, but just at this moment a lack of warmth was not one of her problems!

'Good.' He smiled, utterly at ease with himself in spite of practically being in the nude. 'Then finish that and come and have a swim.'

Apart from the acute discomfort she felt when she first slipped off the robe and sensed Matt's eyes on her—she didn't dare to look at him—the time that followed was full of laughter and fun. Matt was like a kid again in the water, splashing her and grabbing her ankles until she was forced to pay him back in kind, and they had a time of clowning around as well as some serious swimming.

Georgie was not a particularly strong swimmer, but even if she had been she realised quite quickly she wouldn't have been able to compete with Matt. He cut through the water with incredible speed, an automaton clothed in flesh and blood and sinew.

After half an hour or so she climbed out of the pool and sipped her drink again, lying on one of the sun loungers as she watched him cover length after length with effortless ease.

It was another ten minutes before he joined her, and Georgie's stomach muscles clenched as he pulled himself out of the water and strolled over to the lounger at the side of hers. It was one thing lying here supposedly relaxed and cool, sipping elegantly at a drink, when that powerful male body was in the water; quite another when it was a foot or so away.

She had debated whether to clothe herself from head to foot in the robe again when she had first sat down, but with the temperature in the pool area being what it was had decided that would be too ridiculous. And she was a grown woman, she told herself firmly, not some adolescent green behind the ears. Two adults in swimwear was not a prelude to an orgy, even if one of them *was* Matt de Capistrano.

And so she topped up his barely touched drink with a smile when he sat down, exchanged a little small talk and then settled herself back and shut her eyes, commenting this was the most restful evening she had had in a long, long time. She was surprised how well she lied.

She didn't know what she expected in the minutes that followed her declaration, but after a little while she dared to open her eyes enough to slant a quick glance at the side of her.

Matt was lying back on his lounger too, apparently perfectly relaxed, his eyes shut and the big body stretched out and still damp from the water. Georgie frowned. He hadn't made a move on her at all, hadn't even tried to kiss her. And then she felt her face flame at her own inconsistency. She didn't want him to! Of course she didn't. What on earth was the matter with her anyway?

'David and Annie will have the best birthday party ever here,' she said quietly as she sat up and reached for her glass.

'Good.' He didn't move or open his eyes.

'It's really very kind of you to allow your home to be invaded by a host of strangers, especially as most of them will be screaming infants.'

'My pleasure.'

What was the matter with him, for goodness' sake?

Georgie's irritation was totally unfair and she knew it, which made it all the more aggravating. Suddenly the desire to talk, to find out more about the enigmatic individual at the side of her was strong. There was a whole host of questions burning in her brain, and all of them much too personal. She brushed back a strand of silky blonde hair from her cheek and swallowed hard, before she compromised with, 'Do you manage to spend much time at your home in Spain?'

He opened his eyes then, the piercing gaze focusing on her for a moment before he sat up and reached for his own glass, draining the last of the pink liquid before he said, 'Not as much as I would like. My sister's last child is three months old and I have seen him only twice, although this last period has been a particularly difficult one business-wise, with a complicated takeover here in England. Fortunately the Spanish side of things is flowing easily at the moment, and with my brother-in-law at the helm out there I know I have someone I can trust to oversee things for me.'

'Do you have any family from your mother's side here in England?' she asked carefully.

'An uncle.' He swung his legs over the side of the lounger to face her and her senses went into hyperdrive. 'He and my father started the English side of the business with my English grandparents, who are now dead, although my uncle chooses to do less and less these days. He prefers to travel and as he never married and has no ties he is something of a free spirit.' It was wry, and Georgie got the impression not wholly acceptable.

She wanted to ask about Pepita; why he didn't have an English secretary here in England for a start. She had sensed a closeness between Matt and the beautiful Spanish woman that went beyond the bounds of a working relationship, although she could be wrong. But she didn't think so. She hesitated, not knowing how to put it. 'Is…is Pepita's ankle any better?' she asked lamely.

'Yes, I think so.'

It was dismissive and perversely made Georgie all the more determined to continue.

'Does she travel with you back and forwards to Spain?' she asked in as neutral a voice as she could manage, just as a door at the far end of the huge room opened and Rosie called out, 'Dinner in fifteen minutes, Mr de Capistrano.'

'Thank you, Rosie.' He rose as he spoke, holding out a hand to Georgie as he said quietly, 'No doubt you will want to shower before dinner; you should find all you need in the changing room.'

Had he purposely not answered her, or had the question been lost in Rosie's ill-timed interruption? Georgie wasn't sure but the moment had gone anyway. She looked up at him, but before she could take his hand he said, his voice silky smooth now, 'I do not bite, Georgie,' as he bent down and pulled her to her feet.

For a heart-stopping moment she was held against his muscled chest, her hair tousled and her cheeks pink, and she knew he was going to kiss her. So it came as a drenching shock when she was put firmly to one side and Matt's voice said coolly, 'You'll find the towels to one side of the shower cubicle.'

The *towels*? She tried with all her might to show no reaction at all when she said politely, 'Thank you,' before she scurried away, grabbing the robe as she went.

Had he known she expected him to kiss her? Probably. She groaned softly as she stood under the deliciously warm water in the shower after lathering herself with an expensive-smelling body shampoo. Very probably. He was an experienced man of the world; reading a woman's body signals was as natural to him as breathing. But he had shown her he didn't kiss a woman because she indicated she was available, only when he was ready to do so.

She groaned again before taking herself in hand. But she wasn't available, she *wasn't*. She might have suffered a momentary aberration but that was all it had been.

She lathered her hair with the shampoo quickly before rinsing down and drying herself with one of the huge fluffy bath sheets. On the wooden shelf which ran under the mirror along one wall there was every available cream and lotion known to man, along with a display unit holding a vast array of cosmetics, including nail varnish, combs and brushes in unopened packages, lipsticks and anything else a beautician might need.

Georgie ignored it all, drying her hair quickly before she slipped on her own clothes and surveyed herself in the mirror. Without even her customary touch of mascara she looked about sixteen, but that suited her! She scowled at the small slim figure staring back at her. She couldn't compete with the sort of glamorous, dazzling women he was used to and she didn't intend to try, she told herself fiercely, as a beautiful face with slanted ebony eyes flashed across the screen of her mind.

Matt was waiting outside for her when she stepped out of the changing room, looking dark and foreign against the light surroundings. His eyes roamed over her freshly scrubbed face for a moment and then he seemed to echo her previous thoughts when he said softly, 'Sweet sixteen and never been kissed. Although you have, haven't you? Been kissed. Did you respond to him like you respond to me, Georgie?'

'Who?' His previous attitude had lulled her into a false sense of security, she realised now, which was probably what this master strategist had had in mind.

'This man you will not talk about,' he answered with gross unfairness, considering he had closed up like a clam about his own past.

She stared at him for a moment, feeling out of her depth, and then tossed her head slightly as a surge of anger swept away the weakness. She opened her mouth to tell him to mind his own business but he was too quick for her, bending swiftly as his arms went about her and he started to kiss her.

'Let me go, Matt.' She struggled but only briefly, her movements accentuating the softness of her shape against the hard angles of his body, that supremely male body she had had to fight not to ogle for the last hour.

'Why?' He lifted his head but only after he had clasped her face and kissed her until she was gasping.

'Because you said you'd be good,' she managed breathlessly.

'Oh, I am good, Georgie, I promise,' he said with a wicked twist of his lips. 'If nothing else I'm good.'

'You know what I mean.' She was flushed and excited and desperately trying to hide the evidence of her own arousal.

That she'd failed miserably became obvious when he brushed a tantalising finger down the soft slope of one breast and up again. She was swollen and aching, the nipple hard and tender, and as her breath caught in her throat he smiled again. 'You're going to continue to fight me?' he murmured mockingly. 'Why, when you know this can only have one conclusion?'

The Julia Bloomsbury philosophy again. I want therefore I must have. The grating quality of the thought stiffened her back and gave her the strength to jerk away from him, her voice holding a harsh note as she said, 'Matt, there is no way—*no way*—I would sleep with a man I've only known for a few days. I'm not made that way.'

'How long would you have to know a man, my innocent?' he asked smoothly, watching her with gleaming eyes.

Oh, this was crazy; she was getting in deeper and deeper here.

'I don't know.' She shrugged, her face straight and her eyes unhappy. 'A long time.'

'Time is relative.' His mouth was tilting with amusement. And then suddenly his attitude changed, his head nodding as he said, soberly now, 'But I like this in a woman, the ability to hold herself with some value. This is good.'

'It is?' She eyed him uncertainly. She didn't trust him an inch.

'But yes.' His hand reached out and lifted a lock of her hair, allowing it to fall back into place strand by strand as it fanned her face with silky gold. 'Man is the hunter. Did you not know this?'

'Maybe long ago before we became civilised,' she agreed warily.

'I am not civilised, Georgie.'

He didn't appear to be joking and she wasn't altogether sure she disagreed with the statement anyway. The veneer of civilisation sat very lightly on Matt's dark frame; he was dangerous and alien and had more than a little of the barbarian about him.

And then he flung back his head and laughed, the first real laugh she had heard from him, before he said as he met her eyes again, 'You frown at me when I try and make love to you and you frown at me when I agree I must not. What can I do to please you?'

He was laughing at her again and the mockery enabled her to say, her voice very cool, 'Why not try to be a friend first and foremost, or is that too radical a concept for you to take on board?'

'You want friendship from me?' he asked, his eyes on her full soft lips.

'That's beyond your capabilities?' she mocked tauntingly.

'With your brother, no.' He let his gaze take in her creamy skin, the small firm breasts and slender waist, and his voice was dry when he added, 'But you are not a six-foot male, Georgie.'

'It's friendship or nothing.' She sounded much firmer than she felt, she thought with some satisfaction, considering inside she was a quivering mess. She didn't have the first idea what made Matt tick, but she did know it would be emotional suicide to have an affair with him. She would be leaving Robert's office soon but, Matt being Matt, he would still arrange things so he could see her, at least while Robert was involved businesswise with him. This way, with certain ground rules in place, she would have some protection—whether from Matt or her own desire she wasn't sure. Whatever, she needed something!

'Then I agree.' His capitulation was too quick and too easy to be believable.

'Just friends,' she reiterated distrustfully.

'If this is what you want, Georgie.' The way he said her name never failed to set the juices flowing.

Her heart squeezed a little and her voice was all the more firm when she said, 'It is.'

'Then let us go into dinner and celebrate finding each other—as friends,' he murmured silkily. 'Yes?'

She nodded doubtfully. How was it, she asked herself silently, that instead of a victory this felt more like a defeat?

* * *

The dinner was absolutely wonderful, and Georgie found in spite of her racing heart—which just wouldn't behave itself—she enjoyed every mouthful. Goat's cheese, pepper, radicchio and pine nut salad for starters, followed by ravioli of lobster with a red pimento sauce and then chocolate and pear roulade. As she finished the last mouthful of dessert she looked at Matt, seated opposite her across a table resplendent with crystal and silver cutlery in a dining room which was all wood beams and antique furniture and flowing white silk voile curtains, and said, her tone awestruck, 'Do you always eat like this?'

He grinned at her. 'If I was trying to get you into my bed—which now of course I am not,' he clarified meekly, 'I would say, yes, of course, Georgie. As it is…' He allowed a moment or two to elapse. 'You are my friend, yes? And friends do not embroider the truth. So I have to say that I asked Rosie to make something of an effort tonight, although she is an excellent cook and always feeds me well.'

Georgie was still reeling from the grin, which had mellowed the hard face and made him appear years younger, and it took her a moment or two to smile back and make a light comment. He was *dangerous* and never more so than when he was pretending not to be, like now. Or was he pretending? As the evening continued and they had coffee in the exquisitely furnished room Matt had had turned into a drawing room and which overlooked the rolling landscaped gardens at the front of the house, she wasn't sure.

He was relaxed and amusing and the perfect host, and he didn't put a foot—or a hand—wrong. When she made noises about going home just after eleven o'clock he jumped up immediately without any ploys to detain her, and the drive home was uneventful. He saw her to Robert's door, lifted her chin and kissed her fleetingly on the tip of her nose and returned to the car without demur, leaving her standing on the doorstep long after the Lamborghini had disappeared into the night.

Whether it was the wine she had imbibed alone at dinner—Matt had been drinking mineral water after the one cocktail he had allowed himself, due to the fact he intended to drive her home—or the fact that it was the end of an emotionally exhausting day, Georgie didn't know, but she suddenly felt utterly drained.

It was an effort to mount the stairs and get into bed, and she fell asleep as soon as her head touched the pillow, but after a few hours' deep sleep she awoke, knowing Matt had been in her dreams. She lay quietly in the room she shared with Annie, her mind going over all she and Matt had said and done, and she couldn't even think of going back to sleep.

He was in her mind, in her head... She stared into the shadows caused by the burgeoning morning light as her heart thudded at the thought of all that had happened in such short a time, and again the sense of danger enveloped her. And it warned her—more effectively than any spoken words could have done—that she had to be very careful not to let him into her heart too.

Georgie had cause to think, over the next few weeks, that she had grossly exaggerated everything that morning after she had first had dinner with Matt.

As the days passed—the twins' party being the sort of success that would be talked about for years afterwards by their envious friends—and May merged into a blazing hot June, Matt seemed to have inveigled himself into the position of family friend with very little effort.

In spite of there being some sort of hiccup with regard to the starting date of his contract with Robert, he had insisted on financing the hire of extra men and machinery for another job which Robert had won in the meantime and which he would have been unable to accept but for Matt's magnanimity. The two men seemed to have more in common than Georgie would have thought, and it wasn't uncommon for Matt to call round for a coffee or a meal once or twice a week now, when he was always greeted rapturously by Annie and David.

Georgie had left Robert's employ as she'd planned and was now working for a temping agency at double the money Robert could afford, with the knowledge she could take time off in the children's school holidays without feeling she was putting pressure on Robert in his office. Consequently she was not privy to the ins and outs of what was happening with his business, but Robert himself had assured her that the very tasty contract with Matt was still on but just delayed a while due to a few problems with the planners.

'Couldn't have worked out better, actually,' Robert had said when he'd first broken the news in the middle of May. 'This way, with Matt agreeing to lend me the money to finance the Portabello job, we can do that through the next two or three months and then have Matt's job round about September onwards when it's often slack. We've never been busier, Georgie.'

And that was helping him come to terms with Sandra's loss. Georgie nodded to the thought as she fixed the children's breakfasts one baking hot Saturday morning towards the end of June. Which was good, very good. And he was taking more time out to be with the twins in spite of being so busy, and that was even better. He was on an even keel again, Annie and David too, and she had to admit all this was due in no small part to Matt de Capistrano. So why, knowing all this, and accepting Matt now seemed to have done exactly what she had asked and relegated her to friend status and nothing more, was she becoming increasingly dissatisfied and on edge with the status quo?

Did he see other women? She paused for a long moment, staring blindly out of the kitchen window at the sun-scorched grass, before shaking herself mentally and going to the door, whereupon she called the twins, who had been playing in their tree-house since first light, due to the muggy heat in the bedrooms which made sleep difficult. Of course he would.

She dished up the pancakes loaded with lemon and sugar which were the twins' treat every Saturday morning when there was a little more time for a leisurely breakfast, and after going to the foot of the stairs called Robert down too.

He'd be bound to carry on with his social life as normal, she told herself, her mind functioning quite independently of her mouth as she joined in the small talk between Robert and the twins now and again. He had certainly made no attempt to seduce her! Friends she had said and friends they were—he probably viewed her as a female Robert. She glanced at her brother's big square face and sighed inwardly. Perhaps she needed a holiday?

After cooking more pancakes for the other three and serving gallons of freshly squeezed orange juice, Georgie eventually had the house to herself after Robert carted the twins off to their swimming lesson.

She glanced at the kitchen table loaded with dirty dishes and the huge bowl on the worktop which still held some pancake mixture and sighed again. Once she had cleared up in here, the house was waiting for its weekend cleaning session, and there were the beds to change and the fridge to defrost... Life seemed a never-ending cycle of work and more work these days. She grimaced at the maudlin self-pity even as she reiterated, I'm twenty-three, not eighty-three. I want to enjoy life, feel free again, have some fun!

'Oh, stop it!' Her voice was harsh and she was suddenly horrified at her selfishness. 'Think of Robert and the kids, for goodness' sake. What's the matter with you?'

'I have it on good authority that it is the first sign of madness to talk to yourself.'

Georgie jumped so violently as the deep male voice sounded from the doorway behind her that the last of her orange juice shot up in an arc over the table.

'Matt!' She spun round, her hand to her breast, to see him standing big and dark behind her. 'You scared me to death,' she accused breathlessly.

He looked good, very good, but then he always did, she thought ruefully. But today, clothed in light grey cotton trousers and an opened-necked cream shirt, he looked especially good. Or perhaps she was just especially pleased to see him? That thought was too dangerous to pursue, and so she said, forcing a cross note into her voice. 'Why do you creep up on folk like that?'

'I wasn't aware I *was* creeping,' he said with amiable good humour. 'I met Robert and the children on the drive and Robert opened the door for me. He called to you.'

'Did he?' She had been so lost in her own dismal thoughts it would have taken more than her brother's voice to rouse her. 'Well, what do you want?' she asked ungraciously, suddenly aware of how sticky and hot she had got bending over a hot hob.

They looked at each other for a second, his grey eyes pinning her as they darkened and narrowed, and Georgie found she was holding her breath without knowing why.

'A pancake?' His gaze moved to the remaining mixture in the bowl.

A pancake? She found she was staring at the dark profile

stupidly and had to swallow hard before she could say, 'I'm
sure Rosie has given you breakfast.'

'As it happens she has not,' he answered almost trium-
phantly. 'She has gone with her husband to visit relatives
in Newcastle for the weekend. I had some toast and coffee
earlier but I was in the pool at five this morning and it has
given me the appetite.'

It wasn't often he made a mistake in his excellent
English and on the rare occasions he had Georgie hadn't
liked what it had done to her heart. She didn't like it now,
and to cover the flood of tenderness she said abruptly, 'Sit
down, then.' He sat, and, chastened by his obedience, she
added, 'I suppose the heat made you unable to sleep?'

He didn't answer immediately, and as she turned to look
at him she read the look in his eyes and flushed hotly as
he said, very drily, 'This…friend thing carries certain pen-
alties, does it not?'

'I wouldn't know,' she lied firmly.

He slanted a look at her from under half-closed lids and
her colour rivalled that of a tomato. 'I'll see to the pancakes,' she snapped tightly.

'Thank you, Georgie.' It was meek and most un-Mattish.

Fifteen minutes later Matt had demolished three pancakes, a further two rounds of toast and two pint mugs of
black coffee, and Georgie was trying to fight the immense
satisfaction she felt in seeing him sitting at her kitchen table.

'You have given me breakfast; I intend to give you
lunch.' She had been washing the dishes at the sink and as
he turned her round to face him she kept her wet hands
stretched out at the side of her as she said, 'Matt, please, I
have to finish these and then start upstairs. I've masses to
do and—'

'No.' He put a reproving finger on her lips. 'You're having a break. I've already told Robert you won't be back until later tonight.'

'Excuse *me*!' She glared at him. 'You can't just muscle in and tell me what to do. I need to see to the bedrooms.'

'I could tell you exactly what you need to see to in the bedroom of one particular individual who isn't a million miles away, but we won't go into that now,' Matt said smoothly.

'Matt—'

'I know, I know…friends.'

The sexual knowledge in the dark grey eyes was in danger of stripping away all her carefully erected defences and exposing her deepest desires, and Georgie felt mesmerised as she stood before him. Why could he always *do* this? she asked herself crossly. It wasn't fair.

He was holding her lightly on the shoulders, his fingertips warm through the thin material of the old cotton top she had pulled on first thing, and, in spite of everything she had said to Matt and to herself, at this very moment in time Georgie knew she wanted him to respond to her secret need. This wanting him had got worse through the last weeks, not better. It was with her every minute she was awake and it haunted her sleep to the point where she felt exhausted every morning.

She didn't know where an affair with Matt would take her; certainly he wouldn't be content with the fumbling petting she had allowed with Glen. It would be all or nothing with Matt. The only trouble was, 'all' in his case meant full physical intimacy and little else; 'all' in her case would be a giving of her heart and her soul as well as her body.

The thought freed her locked limbs and gave her the strength to step back away from him as she said, her voice very even and controlled despite the turmoil within, 'What did you have in mind for today?'

'A drive into the country, lunch at a little pub I know and then an afternoon relaxing at home by the pool. Rosie has left dinner for us; she's decided you are far too thin and need feeding up,' he added provocatively.

'Too thin?'

'I, on the other hand, think you are just right,' he said softly. 'For me, that is.'

Yes, well, she wasn't in a fit mental state to pursue that particular avenue. 'I'll have to shower and change.'

'I can wait.' There was a hungry fullness to his mouth that stirred her senses. 'I'm getting quite good at it,' he added drily.

'I won't be long.'

'Take all the time you want, Georgie.' He was wearing a sharp lemony aftershave that turned into something incredible on his tanned skin, and her heart went into hyperdrive when he added silkily, 'You are worth waiting for.'

Oh, boy, he was one of his own! Georgie didn't know if she was annoyed or amused as she hurried up to the room she shared with Annie and stripped off her sticky clothes. She didn't linger under the shower and her hair only took a few minutes to blowdry into a silky veil to her shoulders, so it couldn't have been more than a quarter of an hour before she had dressed again in a light white top and flimsy summer skirt, applying just a touch of mascara to her thick eyelashes before she made her way downstairs again.

However, the man who was sitting waiting for her at the kitchen table looked to have aged about ten years.

'Matt?' She was horrified at the change in him. 'What's the matter?'

'I've just had a phone call.' He gestured vacantly at his mobile phone which was lying in front of him on the table. 'It's my mother.'

'Your mother?' Oh, no, no.

'My sister...my sister's with her now, at the hospital. She found her collapsed and virtually unconscious, doubled up with pain.'

'Oh, Matt.' She didn't know what to do or say. His voice had been raw, and in the last few minutes worry and anxiety had scored deep lines in his face. Appalled, she murmured, 'You must go to her of course. What can I do to help?'

'What?'

He was clearly in shock, and Georgie saw his hands were trembling. She couldn't believe how it made her feel and it was in that second—totally inappropriate in the circumstances, she thought afterwards—that she realised how much she loved him. And it was love. Deep, abiding, once-in-a-lifetime love. As different from the puppy love she had felt for Glen as chalk from cheese. But she couldn't dwell on this catastrophe now.

She watched Matt take a deep breath and straighten his shoulders, and his voice was more normal when he said, 'I had better phone the airport. And my uncle, I need to let him know, and he'll have to hold the fort here.'

'I'll come with you.' She didn't even think about it; it was the natural thing to do somehow.

'To the airport? There's no need, really—'

'To Spain,' she cut in calmly. 'You need company at a time like this and we're friends, aren't we? Friends make time for each other.'

'To Spain?' There was a moment of silence and she saw he was struggling to take in what she had said. 'But your work, the twins—'

'I'm temping, so work is not a consideration. As for the twins; they have their father.' She eyed him steadily. 'And each other.' She was repeating the words he had said to her weeks earlier but neither of them were aware of it.

'You would do this? Come to Spain with me?' he asked somewhat bewilderedly.

Spain. The ends of the earth. Planet Zog! 'Of course.'

'Why?'

Because I love you with all my heart and all my soul and all my mind and all my strength. 'Because it might make things a little easier to have a friendly face with you,' she said quietly, 'and you have been terrific to the twins, Robert too, and I've never really said thank you.'

He raked back his hair in a confused gesture that tore at her heart. 'I...I do not know what to say, Georgie.'

At another time, in different circumstances and without the awful possibility of his mother being seriously ill, Georgie would have made plenty of that. The great Matt de Capistrano, silky-smooth operator and master of the silver tongue, at a loss for words? Never!

As it was she lifted up her hand and touched his cheek, careful to keep her eyes veiled so she gave nothing away as she said softly, 'You would do the same for me, Matt, for any of your friends.' And she did believe that, she affirmed silently. He was not a mean-minded man or ungenerous, far from it, and he would go the extra mile without counting the cost. The trouble was, common sense added ruefully, the masculine, ruthless side of him would keep his feelings beautifully under control the whole time. Whereas she...

'If you want to speak to your uncle and make any necessary arrangements, I can phone the airport if you like?' Georgie's voice was brisk now, but then it faltered as he took her hand in his own, holding it against his heart for a moment as he looked down into the deep green of her eyes before he raised the delicate fingers to his lips.

For several moments, moments when the world was quite still and frozen on its axis, she held his gaze. The air itself was shivering with intimacy and the trembling in her stomach threatened to communicate itself to her voice when she murmured, 'It will be all right, Matt, I'm sure of it.'

'Thank you,' he said huskily. He cupped her face in his big hands, kissing her parted lips with a tenderness she would have thought him incapable of. It hurt. Ridiculously, when he was being so nice, it hurt terribly because she wanted it so badly—she wanted *him*. But not just for a few weeks or months, even a year or two. She wanted him for ever, and for everness was an alien concept to him. Oh, what a mess, what a gargantuan mess.

'You're beautiful, Georgie.' His voice caught on her name in the way it always did, making it poignantly sweet. 'Whoever he was, he was a fool. You know that, do you not?'

She nodded. Glen had hurt her terribly at the time, but she knew now he would have hurt her more if she had married him because sooner or later he would have let her down. And it would have been worse, much worse, after they were married, perhaps even with children. He hadn't loved her enough; maybe he wasn't capable of loving anyone enough. Perhaps Julia sensed this and that was why they weren't happy? Whatever, she knew now she hadn't loved Glen enough either. Life with Glen would have been like wearing comfortable old clothes: no highs, no lows, mundane and ordinary. Millions of people the world over settled for just that, admittedly, but she wouldn't be able to do that again. Not now. Not after Matt.

He kissed her once more, and but for the circumstances and the fact that his mother was lying in a hospital bed halfway across the world Georgie was sure she would have leapt on him and ravished him on the kitchen table. As it was she called on every ounce of resolve and carefully removed herself from his hands, her voice a little shaky as she said, 'I'd better phone Robert and let him know what's happening.'

'Wait until I have spoken to the airport. It may be quicker to take a private plane,' Matt said quickly, with a return of his normal authority and command. 'We can land at La Coruna and I will arrange to have a car waiting.'

Georgie nodded silently. She would cope with this—the knowledge that she loved him—she would. As long as he didn't know, everything would be all right. Nothing had changed, not really.

'I'll go and sort out my passport and a few clothes,' she said quietly, scurrying up to the room she shared with Annie. Once in the sunlit room, however, she sank down on the bed for a few moments, staring blankly across the room.

She was committed to being with him for the next few days now, for good or ill, and however things worked out she wasn't sorry she'd offered to go with him. She wanted to see where he had been born, understand that other part of his life and see further glimpses of his complex personality which would be bound to unravel with his family and friends. Had he taken many women to his home town?

Her soft mouth drooped unknowingly for a few seconds and then she raised her head high, narrowing her eyes as she thought, If nothing else, *if nothing else* she would make sure he remembered her a little differently from all the rest. Friendship might not be what she would have chosen, but it singled her out from the crowd!

CHAPTER SEVEN

IT WAS just three o'clock in the afternoon when the private plane Matt had hired landed at La Coruna, northern Spain, where Matt's brother-in-law was waiting for them.

Carlos Molina turned out to be a small man who was as round as he was tall, but he had soft melting eyes, a mouth which looked as though it smiled a lot—but which was strained and tight today—and a shock of unruly curly hair. Georgie liked him immediately.

Matt's influence—and no doubt his wealth—had swept them through Customs in minutes, and once the introductions were over the two men conversed swiftly in Spanish for a few moments before Matt turned to Georgie and said quietly, 'I'm sorry, but Carlos's English is not good and I need to know the details of my mother's collapse.'

'How is she?' Georgie asked softly. They had said little on the journey but when she had taken his hand shortly after departure in a gesture of comfort he had held on to it like a lifeline.

'There is talk of an operation; gall bladder, Carlos thinks.'

'Sí, sí.' Carlos had been trying to follow their conversation, nodding his black head the while. 'You come now the car, she is waiting.'

Georgie hadn't known what she was expecting to see when they left the air-conditioned building, but she supposed her mind had veered towards scorched landscapes and baking hot skies. However, as the silver-blue Mercedes

119

Carlos was driving ate up the miles she was breathless at the scenic beauty unfolding before her eyes.

It was hot, but only as hot as an English summer at its best, and as the car made its way south-west from the airport she had an endlessly changing view of mountains and little villages set in pine-clad hills, traditional-style white-washed villas set among orange and lemon groves, fields of almond, olive and fig trees separated by ancient mellow walls, and houses of golden stone perched on rocky outcrops.

The quality of the light and intensity of colour was totally different from England and overwhemingly beautiful, and they had just passed a village square festooned with market stalls overflowing with produce into the cobbled streets beyond, when Matt said softly at the side of her, 'You like the country of my heart?'

'Like it?' She turned to him impulsively, her face alight. 'It's wonderful, Matt. How can you ever bear to leave it and stay in England for so long every year?'

He smiled slowly. 'England, too, is beautiful,' he said quietly. 'Although I look on Spain as my home I consider myself as English as Spanish, unlike my sister, Francisca. Perhaps it is the names, eh? I was christened after my maternal grandfather Matthew, whilst Francisca took our parental grandmother's first name. Whatever, Francisca is Spanish from the top of her head to the soles of her feet. Is that not right, Carlos?' he said to the man in front of them.

'Sí, sí.' It was very enthusiastic and obviously approving.

Matt turned back to her, his voice dry. 'Carlos is one of the old school,' he said mockingly. 'He likes his woman barefoot and pregnant.'

The way he said the words, in his husky, smoky voice, made Georgie think it wouldn't be such a bad thing after all—if you were Matt's woman, that was—but she forced an indignant note into her voice as she said, 'I'm sure Carlos thinks nothing of the sort. How many children have you got, Carlos?'

He answered in Spanish, and when Georgie glanced enquiringly at Matt, the hard mouth was twisted in a smile as he said softly, 'Hold on to your hat, Georgie. It was eight at the last count.'

'Eight?' She was truly shocked.

'But yes.' He shifted in his seat and as his thigh briefly brushed Georgie's it took all her will-power not to react. 'Spanish men are very virile,' he murmured, straight-faced now. 'Did you not know this?'

She decided not to pursue that path. 'And Francisca wants a big family too?' she asked instead, her cheeks pink but her voice prim.

His smile this time was merely a twitch. 'Of course.'

'That's ideal, then, isn't it?' She turned from him to look out of the window. They were passing a small family, the man leading a plump little donkey which had two curly-haired tots sitting on its furry back and the woman in a long red skirt with a big straw hat on her head, and something about the scene caught at her heart. The children waved to the car and Georgie waved back. They all looked so happy, so relaxed, so *alive*. Life was simple to them, a joy.

And then she caught herself sharply. No. No thinking, no cogitating. One minute, one hour at a time—that was what she'd decided earlier and that was what would see her through the next few days. If she allowed her heart to rule her head and became one of his women it would end badly, for her. As long as she kept that to the forefront of her mind she would be all right.

A few miles further on they passed a crystalline lake,

tranquil under the turquoise sky, and within minutes the
Mercedes turned into a narrow twisting lane off the main
road on which they had been travelling. 'It is better I visit
the hospital with Carlos now,' Matt said quietly, 'and you
must rest and take some refreshments. My housekeeper will
take care of you.'

Even as he was speaking they passed through wide open,
massive iron gates and into a shadow-blotched drive, huge
evergreen oaks forming a natural arch beyond which
Georgie caught a glimpse of magnificent grounds stretching
away into the distance.

'This is your home?' she asked softly.

He nodded. 'Mi Oasis. My Oasis. It has always been
named such and I saw no reason to change it when I bought
the place ten years ago.'

The car had been climbing a slight incline, and now the
drive opened up to reveal an enormous house some hundred
yards in front of them. Unlike most of the houses she had
seen on the journey this one was not whitewashed but built
of mellow, honey-coloured stone and bedecked with ornate
balconies bursting with a profusion of purple, white and
scarlet bougainvillaea, geraniums and pink begonia, and
surrounded by more oak trees. The windows were many
and large, with small leaded squares of glass that twinkled
in the sunlight, and in the middle of the drive in front of
the house a magnificent fountain complete with cherubs
riding prancing horses cascaded into a small stone pool.

'Does this place get a wow, too?' He was smiling as he
spoke, his voice faintly mocking but warm, and Georgie
wrenched her eyes away from the beautiful old house as
she said, 'A double wow, actually.'

'Once you have eaten and bathed you must have a walk
in the gardens at the rear of the house,' Matt said quietly,
his eyes on the front door of the house which had just

opened to reveal a small uniformed maid. 'Pilar will accompany you if you wish.'

'I'd rather explore on my own, thank you,' she said quickly. His voice had been slightly distant and she sensed his mind was focused on his mother now, although his innate good manners had not revealed his impatience to get to the hospital. 'You go, Matt. I'll be fine here until you get back.'

Matt insisted on introducing her to his Spanish housekeeper, Flora, who had appeared beside Pilar within moments, and then escorting her personally to her rooms on the second floor of the three-storey building before leaving, however. 'You will be all right until I return, Georgie?' He touched her cheek as he spoke. 'I have told Flora to bring you a tray in half an hour, once you have had time to shower and change.'

'Thank you.' This wasn't the time to be reflecting on how incredibly sexy he was, and she hated herself for it, but here, in Spain, he seemed ten times more foreign and a hundred times more dangerous. 'And please don't worry about me, Matt. I'll love exploring. The whole point of my coming with you was to be a help, not a hindrance.' And then she forced herself to add, 'That's what friendship is all about, isn't it?'

His thick black lashes hid the expression in his eyes as he responded, after a pause, 'Just so, *pequeña*. Just so.' He bent and touched one flushed cheek with his lips as he spoke, and such was her rush of sexual awareness that Georgie couldn't form the words to ask him what *pequeña* meant before he smiled one last time and closed the door behind him.

'Whew...' She stood exactly where he'd left her for a full minute before she trusted her legs to carry her across the room, whereupon she opened the windows on to the balcony and stepped outside after kicking off her shoes and flexing her aching toes.

The sun-warmed tiles were smooth beneath her bare feet and the ornate iron on the balcony sides was covered in bougainvillaea and lemon-scented verbenas, but it was the scent from the wonderful gardens below, bursting with tropical trees and shrubs and flowers, that flooded her senses. Acres and acres of grounds stretched before her in a dazzling display of colour, and after soaking up the sight for more than five minutes she turned reluctantly into the room behind her. And what a room, what a *suite* of rooms, she thought dazedly.

She was standing in the sitting room, which was the size of Robert's lounge back in England, and the dull rose furnishings embodied two two-seater plump soft sofas, a pine bookcase and a small writing desk and chair, a TV and video and a cocktail cabinet which enclosed a small fridge. The floor was pine and the drapes at the window the same dull rose as the sofas, and this colour scheme was reflected in the big double bedroom which led off the sitting room, although the main colour in there was cream. The bathroom was an elaborate affair in cream marble, and again the towels were in dull rose and gold.

When she had asked, Matt had told her this suite was one of four on this floor, with another four on the floor above. The east wing was given over to the servants' quarters with garages below and an extensive stable block, and the west wing was Matt's private domain which he had promised to show her later.

On the ground floor, which she had not yet seen apart from the baronial hall and huge curving open staircase, there was apparently a drawing room, a sitting room, two other reception rooms, the dining room and breakfast room, and the kitchens.

It was palatial opulence at its best, Georgie thought faintly. Luxurious, grandiose and undeniably stunning. And with more newly built stables behind the west wing, an Olympic-size swimming pool and tennis courts in the grounds... Her mind trailed to a halt. *What was she doing here?* Her, little Georgina Millett from Sevenoaks? This was Rothschild league!

She stood still, her fists pressed to her chest as she panicked big time. The house in England was gorgeous, but this...this was something else. She hadn't realised just how wealthy and powerful Matt was.

After a minute or so of silent hysteria she took a hold of herself. Matt was still Matt. He had been Matt before she had seen this place and he was still Matt. Okay, so he was richer than she'd ever dreamed. She took a deep breath and then gulped hard. But he was the same man who had sat and laughed and joked with the kids in Robert's little dining room over the last weeks, who had taken on a menagerie of decrepit animals to please a frail old lady, who was worried sick about his mother...

And then she gave in to the storm of weeping which had been threatening for the last minutes, had a good howl and dried her eyes. She loved him. She couldn't do anything about it even if every hour that passed emphasised how hopeless it was. Matt was no ordinary man, and she wasn't talking about his wealth now. If he had been dirt-poor he would still have been different, commanding, magnetic. Matt de Capistrano was...well, Matt de Capistrano, she finished weakly. And that said it all. And she'd had to go and fall in love with him...

By the time she had stood under the warm silky water for five minutes Georgie felt refreshed and calmer.

She was still in the big towelling robe which had been hanging in the bathroom when Pilar knocked on the outside door a little while later, and after calling for the little maid to enter she walked into the sitting room and took the tray from her.

There were enough slices of cold beef, pork and ham, green salad, savoury pastries, chopped egg and tomatoes to feed a small army, and Georgie looked at the tray askance, before she raised her eyes to Pilar and said quickly, 'This is lovely but I'll never be able to eat it all.'

'*Perdón, señorita?*'

Georgie repeated herself more slowly, and the little Spanish girl's puzzled frown vanished as she smiled and said, '*Sí, sí.* Do not worry, *señorita.* Señora Flora, she always give b-i-g *raciones*, big—how you say—big snacks, *sí*? Señor de Capistrano, he have the big appetite.'

Georgie nodded thankfully. 'As long as she won't be offended if I leave quite a bit.'

After dressing quickly in a sleeveless ice-blue jersey top and white wide-legged linen trousers Georgie ate a little of the food on the vast tray, washing it down with the glass of red wine that had accompanied the food, before making her way downstairs.

She met Pilar as she reached the bottom of the massive staircase and from the look on the Spanish girl's face Georgie assumed, rightly, she had committed an unforgivable *faux pas* in bringing the tray down herself. She deposited it into Pilar's hands with a smile and told her she was going for a walk in the lovely grounds at the back of the house, and departed swiftly. Her first gaffe and she didn't doubt there would be others. Clearly she didn't know the right way to behave! Unlike Matt's other women, no doubt.

Once in the gardens she paused to look back at the house again. It was so, so beautiful, she thought wonderingly. The decorative iron fretwork, the different shades of the mellow stone, the vivid splashes of crimson, mauve and white from the balconies—she couldn't quite believe she was here!

She explored for a long time, wandering through the grounds and saying hallo to the couple of gardeners she met who had clearly been alerted to her arrival as they greeted her by name.

She was sitting on an ancient wooden seat overlooking an orchard of peach, orange, lemon and cherry trees when she heard her name called, and looked round to see Matt approaching. He hadn't been out of her thoughts for a minute and now she looked anxiously into his dark face. 'Your mother?' she called across the space separating them.

'Brighter than I had expected.' He reached her in a few strides and before she had realised what he was about to do he had pulled her into him, his strong arms slipping round her waist as he moulded her into his hard, firm body, and his chin resting on the top of her head as he nuzzled the warm silkiness of her hair. 'You smell like all the summers I have ever known,' he murmured huskily. 'So fresh, so good.'

How did she answer that? And she wasn't at all sure this embrace could qualify as one of friendship! She rested against him for a moment, simply because she couldn't resist doing so, and then moved back in his arms to say, 'What did the doctors say? Is she going to be all right, Matt?'

'*Sí, sí.*' He shook his head, his voice very smoky as he said, 'Excuse me, Georgie. I have been speaking Spanish all day. Yes, she will be all right I am sure, but she will need the operation. I'm having a specialist flown in from the States tonight and he will operate tomorrow.'

'You are?' How money talked.

'He is a friend of mine and an excellent doctor. My

mother knows and trusts him and it is important she is confident and tranquil.'

Georgie nodded. He looked impossibly handsome and darkly masculine, and the subtle, delicious smell of him was undermining her resolve.

'She would like to meet you.' He was still holding her and didn't seem to notice her attempts to break free.

'She would?' This wouldn't do, she would have to manage more than two words every time she opened her mouth. 'You told her about me then?'

'Yes, I told her about you, Georgie.' His eyes were almost black slits as they narrowed against the evening light which was still very bright. 'I told her you were Robert's sister and that we were friends. This is right, yes?'

'Of course.' And as anguish streaked through her soul she told herself sharply, This is the only way and you know it. You *know* it.

'But I think maybe she guesses it is hard for me to be friends,' Matt continued softly. He traced the outline of her mouth with one finger as he looked down into her face, and when the kiss came it was hot and potent, a raging fire that devoured with dangerous intensity. She had shifted in his arms, momentarily with protest but almost immediately succumbing, even as a little voice in her head berated her for the weakness. After all she had resolved, all she'd determined, he only had to touch her and she was his. The voice was insistent but it couldn't compete with what his mouth and hands were doing, and what she wanted. She loved him so much, so very much.

He was muttering her name and somehow they had come to be lying on the thick grass which was threaded with daisies and forget-me-nots and other bell-like wild flowers. She could feel every muscle, every male contour of his hard shape as intimately as if they were naked, and he wanted her. His body was telling her that all too blatantly.

The heady rush of sensation which had exploded within her was sending waves of pleasure into every nerve and sinew, and his hands were moving erotically and with experienced purpose as they caused her to moan softly in her throat.

Their mouths were joined in a fusion that was a kind of consummation in itself, his tongue thrusting as it invaded her body. His thighs were locked over hers, his hands lifting her buttocks forward to acknowledge his arousal and his heart slamming against his ribcage so hard she could feel it in her own body.

She was returning kiss for kiss, embrace for embrace with an uninhibitedness which would have horrified her if she'd been capable of conscious thought, but it was some minutes before she realised the restraint Matt was showing. He had made no attempt to take their lovemaking to its natural conclusion, indeed she felt he had withdrawn in some way, and this seemed to be borne out when she twisted away and looked into his face, and he let her go immediately. 'What's the matter?' she asked shakily.

'Nothing is the matter except that I cannot trust myself where you are concerned, *pequeña*,' he said ruefully. 'If I had not stopped it would have been impossible to do so in another minute. You understand me?'

'But...I thought...' She didn't know how to go on as the realisation dawned that she had offered herself on a plate to him and *he* had been the one to call a halt.

'That I would take advantage of you at the earliest opportunity?' he asked silkily, his voice losing its softness. 'You came here with me because your heart was moved with sympathy, yes?'

She nodded weakly, because it was all she was capable

of with his big lean body stretched out at the side of her and the taste of him making her head spin.

'And this same sympathy has lowered your defences and made you wish to give me comfort,' he continued quietly. 'This is good, I like this, but when we make love properly, Georgie, it will be for one reason and one reason only. Because you want me as much as I want you and it is the only thing filling your mind and your heart. Not pity or a wish to comfort, not even that the evening is soft with the scent of flowers and there is romance in the air like now.'

Was he *crazy*? Didn't he know how much she wanted him? Not through pity or anything else except good old earthy desire, made all the more powerful because she loved him.

Georgie opened her mouth to tell him of his mistake and then shut it again with a little snap. It wasn't Matt who was crazy, it was her, she told herself silently as cold reason stepped in. She knew in her heart of hearts he would eat her up and spit her out and go on his own sweet way sooner or later, so why on earth was she playing with fire?

'Come.' He rose to his feet with the sinuous grace which characterised all his movements, and held out his hand to help her up. 'We will wander back to the house and have cocktails before dinner. Then we will eat and talk and laugh, and later see the moon rise like a queen in the sky. Yes?'

She took his hand, scrambling to her feet with none of his panache. He had told her he didn't believe in true love and for everness and he was thirty-six years old, not a raw callow youth who didn't know his own mind. But what had made him that way? There had to be something, surely? People didn't just wake up one morning and decide to be that cynical. Would her experience with Glen have sent her down that path if she hadn't met Matt before she had become hardened? Well, she'd never know now, would she? Because she *had* met him.

She smoothed down her rumpled clothes, her cheeks flaming as she fumbled with the tiny mother-of-pearl buttons on her top, several of which were undone.

Matt, on the other hand, appeared perfectly cool and relaxed, as controlled and in charge as ever. There were times, Georgie told herself with silent savagery, when she hated him as much as she loved him, and this was definitely one of those times!

He drew her arm through his as they strolled back to the house through the perfumed warm air, every bird in the world—or so it seemed to Georgie's feverish senses—singing a love song. Matt was chatting easily, filling her in on everything that had happened at the hospital that afternoon and reiterating his mother was bright and cheerful. Which was great, fantastic, Georgie thought ruefully, but how he could think about anything else except what had nearly happened out there, she just didn't know! But then it was just a sexual thing with him, a hunger that required sating. You ate when you were hungry, drank when you were thirsty and bedded a woman when you wanted sexual release. Matt's philosophy on life in a nutshell.

They entered the house though the open French doors of the stately drawing room, which was clearly the way Matt had exited, although Georgie had left the house by the less exalted exit by the kitchens, and he kept hold of her as they walked through the high-ceilinged, cathedral-type splendour into the hall beyond.

'Do you use the drawing room often?' she asked a little weakly. The exquisite furnishings—most of which looked to be priceless antiques—were a little daunting.

'High days and holidays; isn't that what you English say?'

His voice had held a mocking note and now Georgie's was a touch indignant when she said, 'You're English, too.'

'Half-English,' he corrected softly. 'And this makes a difference, yes?'

Oh, yes. She almost missed her footing, although there was nothing to trip over but her own sinful thoughts.

Matt glanced at his watch. 'There's plenty of time before we need to change for dinner for you to come and see my home within my home,' he offered, adding with a mocking twist of his lips, 'And you must consider yourself highly honoured to be asked. It is only by invitation anyone passes into the inner sanctum.'

Georgie didn't return the smile and stared at him steadily. 'Is that true?' she asked quietly.

The teasing look vanished, and Matt answered just as quietly, 'Yes, it is true. And I am chary with the invitations. I value my privacy.'

She could believe that. He might entertain lavishly and have a wide group of friends and acquaintances, but she had learnt Matt de Capistrano was a man who revealed only a little of himself to anyone, and then even that little was jealously monitored.

Georgie walked with him down the hall and watched as he opened the heavy wood door leading to his separate wing. Matt waved her past him, and she found herself in what appeared to be another smaller hall complete with a beautifully worked wrought-iron spiral staircase.

'Come.' He took her hand in his. 'The downstairs first, I think.'

The downstairs first. That meant he intended to show her the upstairs next. And upstairs meant his bedroom.

The hall floor was again wood—honey-coloured oak— and the painted walls reflected this colour but in a much paler hue. Instead of the fine paintings which adorned the main hall, these walls had continuous sheets of bronze-tinted mirror from waist height, and in the last of the day's sunlight slanting in the tall narrow windows on the right-hand side of the hall the space became a place of pure golden light.

Matt opened the door on his left and again stood back for her to precede him.

'Oh, Matt.' Surprised into looking at him, she saw the dark grey eyes had been waiting for her reaction. They were standing looking out over a wonderful indoor swimming pool, beyond which, at the far end of the pool, there were huge palms and plants enclosing several big upholstered loungers and a table and chairs. The end wall consisted mostly of glass, with two large patio doors which opened out onto a walled garden full of flowers and shrubs and trees.

'My gym.' He had been leading her to a door halfway along the pool and now opened it to reveal a well-equipped gymnasium and sauna, complete with showers and toilet facilities.

'It's wonderful.' As he closed the door to the gym again Georgie glanced around her, quite overwhelmed. 'Did you have all this done?'

He nodded. 'I prefer to swim and exercise in the nude,' he stated, without appearing to notice the effect of his words on the colour of Georgie's skin, 'and this would not be…appropriate outside on certain occasions.'

Georgie nodded in what she hoped was a cool, cosmopolitan kind of way and forced the X-rated pictures flashing across the screen of her mind back under lock and key. 'It's very nice,' she said primly, 'and very private.'

'Just so.'

Was he laughing at her? As they walked back into the hall she glanced at his dark face out of the corner of her eye but his expression was deadpan. Not that that meant anything. Not with Matt de Capistrano, she thought resentfully.

'Up you go.' As she climbed the spiral staircase she was terribly aware of Matt just behind her and almost stumbled as she stepped out into the open plan bedroom. She hadn't been expecting his bedroom to be next—she'd assumed that would be at the top of the house—and she certainly hadn't expected it to be so…so— She gave up trying to find suitable adjectives and gazed warily about her.

Again the end wall was all glass, and the huge, soft, round billowy bed, which was easily two and a half metres in diameter, was only slightly raised off the wooden floor, positioned so the occupant had a scenic view across tree tops and the vast expanse of light-washed sky. The left-hand wall was mirrored like the hall had been but this time in a smoky glass to five feet high, at which point shelves holding books, magazines and tapes reached to ceiling height.

A TV was fixed on the right hand wall, next to which the doors of the walk-in wardrobe were open to reveal neatly stacked shelves and racks of suits and other masculine clothing.

A large plump three-seater sofa was standing at the opposite end of the room from the bed, by the side of which was a fridge and a low table holding a coffee machine and cups. On the other side of the sofa there looked to be a well-stocked cocktail cabinet.

The sofa and the duvet, along with the floating voile curtains at the windows, were in a light cream, but the numerous pillows and massive cushions piled on the bed, along with the stack of cushions scattered on the sofa were in unrelenting black cotton.

Altogether it was an uncompromisingly masculine room,

devoid of colour and any feminine frills, and this was reflected in the *en suite* bathroom when Matt opened the door next to the wardrobe to reveal a bathroom of black marble and silver fittings without one plant or feathery fern to soften its elegant, stark beauty.

Georgie stared inside, the subdued lights which had come on automatically when the door was opened, and which were hidden for the most part, emphasising the voyeuristic nature of the gleaming marble and inevitable mirrored wall rising up behind the black marble bath.

Georgie couldn't think of a single coherent thing to say. She was still struggling to come to terms with that incredible bed, which just had to have been built inside the room to Matt's specification, and now to be presented with such unashamed lasciviousness...

She swallowed hard, her throat dry. This was one unrepentant bachelor, she told herself fiercely, everything she had seen this far screamed it, and she ignored it at her peril.

'You do not like these rooms?' He closed the door to the bathroom as he spoke and she was forced to meet the dark piercing gaze trained on her face.

'Like them?' How did she answer that? They were beautiful, magnificent, but they carried their own warning and it was like a slap in the face. But the rooms themselves were out of this world. 'Yes, of course I like them,' she answered after a moment, her voice very even. 'They're extraordinary; the whole house is stunning.'

He surveyed her unblinkingly. 'Never play poker, *pequeña*.'

'What?' She pretended not to know what he meant, to give herself time to get her brain in gear.

He smiled, but it was just a movement of his lips and didn't reach the steel-grey eyes. 'Come and see the top floor,' he said easily, as though he wasn't in the least bothered by what he imagined she was thinking. Which he probably wasn't, Georgie affirmed miserably.

And then she flushed furiously when, instead of moving towards the staircase, he paused for a moment, brushing his lips across her forehead as he murmured, 'The top floor is safer, I promise.'

'Safer?' She tried to ignore what his closeness was doing to her hormones and injected a note of annoyed surprise into her voice. 'I don't know what you are talking about.'

'Sure you don't.' Now the hard, faintly stern mouth was wolfish.

'Matt, I'm telling you—'

And then her voice was cut off and her stomach muscles contracted when his hand followed the curve of her cheek down to her throat. He wasn't holding her, he was barely touching her, and yet his fingers were fire against her skin and she had to stiffen herself against his touch.

'This is what I'm talking about,' he said very softly, 'the chemical reaction that happens whenever we're in ten feet of each other.'

His gaze dropped to her mouth and her lips parted instinctively, as though her body had a mind of its own. She could feel warmth pulsing through her and sensed the tension that was holding his big muscled body taut, and she knew she had to break the moment. That bed, that wonderful, marvellous, voluptuous bed, was too close…

'I'm ready to see upstairs now,' she said in a staccato voice. Chemical reaction he'd said. Just chemical reaction. *What was she going to do?*

CHAPTER EIGHT

THE top floor of Matt's wing was another surprise. A large part of it was given over to a frighteningly well-equipped study, with all the latest technology in use, but behind this area, at the far end of the room, an extended enclosed balcony in the form of a small sitting room gave a bird's eye view stretching into infinity.

Beyond Matt's estate there were rolling hills and countryside and small villages, a dramatic vista which was awe-inspiring.

'Sit down. I'll fix us a drink.'

Georgie nodded her acquiescence, wandering over to the full-length semicircle of windows. 'I don't think I've ever seen a view to match this one,' she said slowly without turning to look at him.

She heard the chink of ice against glass and then was conscious of him just behind her. 'Incredible, isn't it?' he murmured softly.

'Surely all this part of the house didn't have such huge windows when you bought it?' she asked quickly, the scent of his male warmth surrounding her and telling her she had to keep talking.

There was a brief pause and then he said, 'No, it didn't. I had this wing changed to suit my requirements. I like space and light.'

It wasn't what he said but something in his voice, the merest inflexion, which sent pinpricks of awareness flickering down her spine. The almost obsessive demand for spaciousness, the mirrors, the huge windows... 'You're claustrophobic?' She turned to him but it wasn't really a question. And as his eyes narrowed, she reiterated, 'You are, aren't you?'

He shrugged. 'A little.'

A lot, she bet. 'Have you always been so?'

'No, not always.' His voice was dismissive and he made it clear he didn't intend to respond further to the curiosity in her voice when he took her arm and drew her down on to the sofa, handing her a glass of white wine as he said, 'Relax and enjoy the view, Georgie.'

Easier said than done.

She sat, her knees tightly together and her back straight, staring rigidly out across the rolling hills and countryside which merged to a dusky faint mauve on the far horizon. So he had a small chink of weakness in that formidable armour he wore—claustrophobia. And it was indicative of the inner strength of the man that she had known him for many weeks now and had never guessed. She found that thought incredibly depressing.

'Are you ready to tell me about him yet?'

'What?' She had jerked away like a skittish colt before she could collect herself.

'Did he break your heart, Georgie?' he asked gruffly.

This was so *unfair*! He revealed nothing—*nothing*—of himself and yet he expected her to spill everything. She stiffened and then raised her small chin. 'His name was Glen,' she said steadily. 'What was her name?'

'Her?' His eyes went flat and cold.

'Yes, her. There must have been a her.' She was guessing, but everything about his body language told her she'd hit gold. Or ashes, depending on how you looked at it.

'Kiss and tell?' he said harshly.

She blanched at his tone, but she wasn't going to back down now. She was tired of going round in circles, and since the first moment she had laid eyes on Matt she felt that was what she'd been doing. 'Exactly,' she challenged bravely. 'Or aren't you up for it yourself? You just expect me to tell you all, is that it?'

He stared back at her for a long moment as something worked in his hard face which she couldn't read. 'I didn't mean—' He stopped abruptly, dark colour slashing his cheekbones. 'Or maybe I did. Hell, I don't know what I mean.'

The momentary loss of composure pleased her more than words could say. It was a start. If nothing else it was a start, wasn't it?

He drew air in between his teeth in a low hiss, his glittering eyes narrowed on her pale face, and then said coldly, 'You won't like what you hear and it will serve no useful purpose.'

'I'd prefer to be the judge of that,' she said, speaking evenly, not wanting him to guess that part of her was terrified. 'I haven't lied to you, Matt, I've been totally honest since we met.' Her conscience twanged here but she brushed aside the still small voice which questioned why she hadn't told him she loved him. That was different, quite different. It was. 'I've always made it clear I'm not in the market for a casual affair; I don't live my life like that. I know you but I don't know you, and you offer nothing of yourself, not really.'

'Charming.'

'Oh, you've been great to Robert and the twins, don't get me wrong, and you're amazingly generous, but that's just money, isn't it?' she said, looking him straight in the eyes and trying not to dwell on how darkly handsome he looked sitting there, a touch away.

'Which of course is nothing,' he drawled sarcastically.

'No, it's not,' she agreed tersely, suddenly furiously angry with him too. 'Money is great if you've got it and it certainly smoothes the way, but Sandra and Robert had something no amount of cash could buy. And, having seen them, having seen what they had, I would never be content with anything less.'

'It's dangerous to put a relationship on a pedestal like that and rather arrogant to assume you know what their marriage was really like.' It was expressionless and cold. 'You could find yourself following some sort of illusion for the rest of your life and end up with nothing.'

'I saw their ups and downs and know how hard they worked at their marriage to make it the success it was,' Georgie answered tightly, 'and I didn't view it through rose-coloured spectacles, if that's what you're insinuating.'

He stared at her, his black brows drawn together in an angry scowl. 'How are we arguing when I meant this to be—?' He stopped abruptly.

'Cosy and intimate?' she suggested with acid sweetness.

'Relaxing and beneficial.'

Relaxing and beneficial? Yeah, sure! She glared at him, her green eyes stormy, and took a long gulp at the wine to prevent herself from throwing it at him.

From rage he was suddenly grinning and it had the effect of leaving her in no man's land, especially when he said, his voice husky, 'You're a formidable opponent, Miss Millett.'

'Opponent?' She wasn't ready to melt yet. 'I thought we were supposed to be friends, and friends should be able to have healthy disagreements.'

'Right.' He nodded, his mouth quirking at the haughty note in her voice. 'What else are friends allowed to do?'

'Do you mean to tell me you've never had any women friends?' she answered stiffly.

'Not ones with eyes the colour of pure jade and hair of

raw silk,' he murmured softly. 'You've bewitched me, do you know that? You fill my thoughts and you invade my dreams, and all I think about is you.'

It was an unexpected confession and Georgie couldn't quite believe it was real.

'I mean it.' As always he read her face.

He probably did. For now. But now would turn into yesterday and then what would she do? She knew, even without looking too deeply inside herself, that once she gave Matt everything she would never recover from it.

'Her name was Begonia.'

'What?'

He tilted her face towards him, his fingers gentle, and said again, 'You asked her name. It was Begonia.'

She didn't want to know her name. She didn't want to know anything about this woman he had known and cared for. And she wanted to know everything.

'I met her at university, here in Spain,' he said quietly. 'We were together for eighteen months and then it finished.'

Was she beautiful? Had he loved her with all his heart? Had Matt finished it? Where was she now?

'And Glen?' he asked without a change of tone. 'Who was Glen?'

Glen was nothing. Georgie took a deep breath. 'Glen was the original boy next door,' she said carefully. 'I grew up with him once I went to live with Robert and Sandra; his sisters were my best friends for a while. We got engaged and he broke it off a few weeks before the wedding.'

'Why?'

'He found someone else.' He was still holding her face and now she broke the hold, turning away slightly and taking another gulp of wine before she added, 'He went off with his boss's daughter; she was very wealthy or, rather, her father was. They got married a few months later.'

'He was a fool.' It was tender.

'Yes, he was.' She was trying very hard to keep any emotion out of her voice. 'But I realised later—' once I had met you and realised what love was all about '—it would have been a huge mistake.'

'Do you mean that?'

There was a note in his voice she couldn't quite place, and now she raised her eyes to meet the piercing gaze trained on her face and said quietly, 'Oh, yes, it's not bravado. I had hero-worshipped him when we were younger and he could do no wrong in my eyes, so it was an awful shock when he unceremoniously dumped me, but after a while I realised I'd built him up in my head as someone completely different to who he really was. Puppy love, I suppose; certainly blind infatuation. Marriage to Glen would have been a disaster.'

She swallowed hard. She wanted to ask more about this Begonia and now was the time, she might never have another opportunity like this, but could she bear hearing it?

And then the decision was taken out of her hands when the telephone at the side of the sofa began to ring. Matt swore softly as he picked up the receiver, his voice sharp as he said, '*Sí?*'

Georgie could hear it was a woman's voice on the other end of the line and as her senses prickled she wasn't surprised to hear him say, '*Sí*, Pepita,' followed by more Spanish. And his voice was not sharp now.

She rose to her feet, wandering across to the windows with her back towards him and looking out on to the view as her ears strained for every inflexion of his voice.

'I am sorry, Georgie.' As Matt replaced the receiver she turned round slowly, her face showing nothing but polite enquiry. 'That was Pepita. She was anxious for news of my mother.'

'She knows her, then?' She was amazed how calm and matter-of-fact her voice was when the screen of her mind was replaying a picture of the other woman's elegant, red-taloned hand resting intimately on his arm.

He nodded. 'Pepita has been with me for many years,' he said absently. 'She knew my mother well; they are great friends.'

Yes, they would be, because Pepita would have made sure of it. She wanted Matt. Georgie suddenly realised the knowledge had been there in her head from the first morning. Pepita was in love with him. Was he aware of it?

'She was phoning from her car; she is on her way here with some flowers for my mother.'

Right. She wasn't taking them to the hospital or arranging for them to be delivered. She was bringing them here, to Matt's home. 'I wasn't aware Pepita was in Spain,' Georgie said pleasantly. And now she asked the question she had asked once before in England, and never received an answer to, 'Does she travel backwards and forwards with you between England and Spain?'

'Most of the time.' There was the faintest note of mild irritation, as though he didn't want to talk about his beautiful secretary. 'My uncle in England has his own secretary, of course, and the office there is efficient, but I prefer to have Pepita with me for any confidential work.'

He preferred to have Pepita with him. Georgie put the half-full glass of wine down on a small occasional table and gestured at her clothes as she said, 'I'll think I'll go and freshen up before dinner, if that's all right?'

'Of course.'

Yes, it would be 'of course' now Pepita was on her way here. And then Georgie caught at the thought, self-disgust strong. She loathed the destructive emotion of jealousy and she had never been subject to it before. She had to get a handle on this. Matt was a free agent; he could sleep with a hundred women, including his secretary, and she had absolutely no right to object. No right at all...

Georgie hadn't known what clothes to bring with her when she had hastily packed her suitcase earlier that morning in England, but now, standing in her bra and panties in front of the open wardrobe in her room, she blessed the impulse that had made her grab two or three dressy outfits at the last moment. She would bet her life on the fact that Pepita was not going to arrive in anything less than designer perfection, and although her salary couldn't run to Versace or Armani her jade-green silk dress with an asymmetric hemline, the off-the-shoulder three-quarter length pastel cashmere dress and, lastly but not least, the viscose-crêpe minidress in soft charcoal would all hold their own with a designer label.

Her green eyes narrowed on the minidress. The wafer-thin straps on the shoulders and touch of embroidery which followed the neckline took the dress to another dimension once it was on, and her strappy sandals in dark pewter toned perfectly. It wasn't quite so dressy as the other two but that was perfect; she didn't want Pepita to think she had tried too hard. And the material and colour were misty and chimerical, bringing out the colour of her hair and eyes and accentuating the honey tone of her skin.

She had a thick braided bracelet and necklace in silver that she'd worn with the dress at the dinner dance she'd originally bought it for, and apart from two sets of earrings they were the only pieces of jewellery she had brought with her. Fate? She reached for the dress as she nodded at the reflection in the mirror.

She brushed her hair until it hung either side of her face like raw silk, but apart from darkening her thick eyelashes with mascara and applying the lightest touch of peach-coloured lipstick to her mouth she titivated no more, in spite of the picture of a beautifully made-up face and exquisitely enhanced ebony eyes which kept getting between her and the fresh-faced girl in the mirror. She wasn't used to wearing much make-up and she wasn't about to make herself feel uncomfortable. She wasn't a *femme fatale* and there was no point in trying to look like one.

Once she was ready she glanced one more time in the mirror. The three-inch heels gave her slender five feet four inches a boost, but she would never be model material, she decided resignedly. And Pepita must be five foot ten if she was an inch.

But that didn't matter. She frowned the admonition. She was here to give moral support to Matt through a difficult time by way of thanks for all he had done for Robert and the twins. That was all. *That was all.*

She picked her way carefully down the wide curving staircase once she had left her suite of rooms, vitally aware that the last thing she needed was to trip over the unaccustomed high heels and go sprawling from top to bottom. Once in the shadowy hall she came to a halt, however, uncertain of which room Matt would be in.

'*Señorita?*' A uniformed angel in the shape of Pilar appeared from the direction of the kitchens. 'You want the señor, *sí?*'

Oh, yes. Georgie nodded, her hair shimmering as she moved her head. 'I wasn't sure if he was in the drawing room or not,' she proferred tentatively.

'No, no, *señorita*. Is blue room, I think.'

Pilar led the way to one of the other reception rooms, opening the ornately carved door for Georgie and standing to one side for her to enter. And in the split second it took for Georgie to look into the room beyond she saw the couple standing by the window draw apart, Matt turning to face her as he said coolly, 'Georgie, we have been waiting for you. Come and have a cocktail.'

They had been embracing. Georgie tried to think of something to say and failed utterly, so she merely walked into the beautiful room which was furnished in shades of blue with as much aplomb as she could muster, forcing herself to smile as Pepita extended a languidly limp hand and said flatly, 'It is nice to see you again. I hope your brother is well?'

'Hallo, Pepita. Yes, Robert's fine.' Her voice was steady and even friendly, but she felt as though she had just received a heavy blow in the solar plexus. *They had been embracing*; Pepita's hands resting against the cloth of his dinner jacket and her head lifted up to meet Matt's downward bent one. Had they actually kissed? It was a pose which suggested they had but she hadn't seen that. Whatever, this wasn't your average working relationship!

Matt was pouring her a drink, and as he handed her the fluted glass his eyes roamed hungrily all over her for a few vital seconds, but his voice was contained when he said, 'You look lovely tonight, Georgie.'

'Thank you.' She smiled and took the drink as though she hadn't a care in the world, but even though she wasn't looking directly at Pepita now the image of the beautiful Spanish woman was imprinted on her mind.

As she'd suspected, Pepita was dressed to kill. The sleeveless silk dress with a deep V neck in dark scarlet was the ultimate in clingy sultriness and Pepita's figure was amazing; the high red sandals with studded ankle straps she was wearing showed her long slim legs off to perfection.

Had Pepita known she was staying with Matt? Georgie

rather suspected not. She also had a sneaking suspicion her presence was as welcome as an old flame at a wedding.

It soon became clear Matt had invited Pepita to stay for dinner and Georgie supposed—if she was being honest— he could have done little else, but it was a terrible evening as far as Georgie was concerned.

Pepita had obviously decided to sparkle, and she accomplished this with a brittle effervescence that had Georgie wanting to punch the other woman on the nose for most of the time. Pepita was never actually rude, but she managed to introduce people and situations Georgie had never heard of into the conversation, constantly emphasising Georgie was the odd one out. It was annoying, it was very annoying, but other than cause a scene Georgie could do little about it, and a scene was quite out of the question with Matt's mother lying ill in hospital with a forthcoming operation looming.

The food Flora had prepared was wonderful and the dining room was like something out of a Hollywood movie, but Georgie could have been eating cardboard for all it registered. Matt himself said little—it was difficult for anyone other than Pepita to get a word in, and Georgie could see how the other woman kept her slim figure because she never stopped talking long enough to swallow anything— and Georgie got the impression once or twice he was almost bored. Or perhaps he was regretting bringing her with him now Pepita had turned up?

This thought occupied her all through Flora's wonderful dessert of strawberry granita with a liqueur muscat chantilly. When she thought about it, Georgie reflected she had left him no choice but to let her tag along. She had *announced* she was accompanying him rather than asking him. Other than being blatantly rude, she hadn't left him with any option, had she? Her ears began to burn with embarrassment and her mouth went dry with panic.

She should never have come. This had been a huge, huge mistake and Pepita's presence confirmed it. Probably the Spanish woman spent most of her evenings with him here when they were both in Spain? And Pepita was only one of many glamorous women who would vie to be noticed by him. What on earth had she been thinking of to push herself on him the way she had? What must he be thinking?

She suddenly felt very naïve and stupid, all the confidence the lovely dress had given her evaporating away, but in the next instant she raised her chin a fraction, her eyes narrowing slightly. She was blowed if she would give Pepita the satisfaction of even an inkling of what she was thinking. Cool, calm and collected—that was her mask for the evening and she would wear it even if it killed her, and to the bitter end too. No slinking away or pleading a headache, even if that was in actual fact a reality. But then Pepita's chatter was enough to give a deaf man a headache! It continued all through their after-dinner coffees and brandy. By the time eleven o'clock chimed Georgie was just thinking she couldn't survive another minute without screaming, when Pepita rose to her feet, her movements slow and languid.

'Thank you so much for a lovely dinner, Matt.' She smiled and touched his arm as she spoke—he had risen with her—and Georgie reflected, with a painful squeeze of her heart how good they looked together. 'Do give your mother my love along with the flowers? And if there is anything, *anything* I can do you know you only have to ask.'

'Thank you, Pepita.' He turned to Georgie, holding out his hand and pulling her to her feet whereupon he drew her into the side of him as he said easily. 'We'll see you out.'

Georgie knew she had turned lobster-red but she couldn't help it; there had been an intimacy about both the gesture and the words she was sure Matt hadn't meant, but certainly it had hit Pepita on the raw if the stone-hard glint in the other woman's onyx eyes as she met Georgie's was anything to go by.

Matt kept hold of her as they all walked into the hall, and once he had opened the front door and they all stepped outside he didn't seem to notice her subtle attempts to disentangle herself.

Pepita was driving a bright red Porsche—which somehow seemed to sum up the evening as far as Georgie was concerned—and whether by design or accident showed a great deal of smooth tanned leg as she slid into the driver's seat. And then the car was pulling away with a flamboyant hoot of the horn and within a moment or two they were alone.

'Nice car.' Georgie had finally managed to extricate herself by pretending to fiddle with the strap of her sandal a moment before, and now she straightened, her voice cool.

'Yes, it is.' His face was in shadow and she couldn't see the expression in his eyes.

'Does she live near?' She had hoped her voice would sound polite and conversational and heard the edge to it with a feeling of despair.

'Quite near.'

'That's very convenient.' The black brows rose and she added quickly, 'For work purposes, I mean.'

'Of course,' he agreed pleasantly. There was a second's silence and then he horrified her by saying evenly, 'There is no need to be jealous, Georgie.'

''*Jealous?*'' Matt was the second person she wanted to hit on the nose that evening and her response shocked her because she was normally a very non-violent person. 'I think you flatter yourself, Matt,' she bit out with caustic venom.

'Possibly.'

'And I can assure you I don't have a jealous bone in my body!'

'A very delectable body too.'

She glared at him, so angry she didn't trust herself to speak for a moment. How dared he suggest she was jealous of Pepita? she asked herself furiously, ignoring how she had felt for the last few hours. The ego of the man was colossal! No doubt he'd thoroughly enjoyed the thought he had two women panting after him all evening! Well, he could go and take a running jump, the arrogant so-and-so.

'Pepita's mother—when she was alive; she died three years ago—was my mother's closest friend,' Matt said from behind her as they turned into the house. 'I was ten years of age when Pepita was born and I have watched her grow from an infant.'

How cosy. And that explained the hungry look in Pepita's ebony eyes, did it? Who did he think he was kidding? 'You don't have to explain anything to me,' Georgie said tightly.

'I am not doing it because I have to,' he said softly, catching her arm and turning her round once he had shut the door, 'but because I want to. I do not wish any misunderstanding between us.'

She stared at him in the dimly lit hall, her green eyes huge with doubt.

'Pepita is like family,' Matt said quietly, 'that is all.'

She wanted to believe him, and the fervency of the wanting carried its own warning. He was pure enigma; she didn't understand him at all and she never would. For the moment she was someone he wanted, a passing obsession, but he was used to women who were content to have fun with him for however long it took for the affair to burn itself out and then leave his life as gracefully as they had entered. And she didn't have it in her to be like that. She'd leave wailing her head off and clinging hold of his legs! She loved him.

'Like I said, Matt, you don't have to explain anything to me,' she said steadily, her voice quiet now. 'I came here because I thought it might help to have a friend with you at a difficult time. That's all.' Which was probably the most stupid thing she had done in her life.

'You are very good to your friends, Georgie.' He had bent and wrapped his arms around her before she realised what was happening, his lips seeking hers hungrily, possessive and devouring.

If someone had told her just two or three minutes before that she would be kissing him back she would have laughed at them, but that was exactly what she was doing as a flood of passion engulfed her. Her arms had wound round his neck and her body was pressed close to his, and she could no more have stopped her response to him than ceased breathing.

He didn't draw away until she was trembling and weak in his arms, and then his voice carried a smoky mocking note when he murmured, 'Very good.'

This was just a game to him. It gave her the strength to take a step backwards and say determinedly, 'Goodnight, Matt.'

'Goodnight, Georgie.'

She had half expected him to try and detain her but he didn't move as she walked to the staircase, and she was halfway up the stairs when his voice arrested her. 'I would like you to come with me to the hospital tomorrow and meet my mother.'

She remained perfectly still for the split second it took

to compose her face, and then she turned, one hand holding the smooth carved handrail as she said lightly, 'I'd like to meet her.'

It didn't mean anything, she warned herself firmly as she continued up the stairs. Not a thing. He obviously felt obliged to introduce her after she had come all the way from England, and no doubt his mother would think it odd if he didn't. Nevertheless the misery of the evening spent in Pepita's company was suddenly all gone and she all but floated along to her suite, walking through the sitting room and straight into the bedroom where she stood and looked at the bright-eyed girl in the mirror. 'Careful, Georgie.' She touched her lips, which were moist and swollen from his kisses, with the tip of one finger. 'He hasn't made any promises except that he doesn't believe in love or commitment.'

She stood at the mirror for a moment more, her eyes searching her flushed face as though the answer to all her confusion was there, and then sighed deeply, turning away and kicking off the sandals before making her way into the bathroom.

She would run herself a warm bath and lie and soak for half an hour at least; she was far too het-up to go to sleep yet. And she would not think of Matt at all. She wouldn't. These few days were a brief step out of time and that was the way she had to look at them. Pepita, the love affair that had gone wrong for him at university, his other women—she would go mad if she tried to sort it all out in her head tonight. He was one of those men whose dark aura engulfed everyone and everything it came into contact with, and she couldn't trust herself any more than she could trust him.

She walked back into the bedroom thoughtfully once the bath was running, taking off her clothes and donning a towelling robe before wiping off her mascara with her eye-make-up removing pads.

She must phone Robert tomorrow and assure him everything was all right; he had sounded worried when she'd said she was going to Spain with Matt although he had calmed down once she had explained about his mother. But she knew her brother had still been unhappy about the situation when she had put down the phone. Had he guessed how she felt about Matt? No, not Robert. Intuition wasn't his strong point. Perhaps he just wanted to warn her from getting involved, let her know that men like Matt de Capistrano were not the roses round the door type. Well, she knew that.

She narrowed her eyes as she padded back into the bathroom and turned off the taps. Yes, she knew that all right—in her head. So why was her heart still hoping for something different?

CHAPTER NINE

WHETHER it was the warm bath or the fact that Georgie had expelled enough nervous energy in the last twenty-four hours to exhaust ten women, she didn't know, but she awoke the next morning after a deep refreshing sleep that had—as far as she could recall—been dreamless. It was Pilar who woke her, placing a steaming cup of coffee on the bedside cabinet as she said gently, '*Señorita*, you sleep well, *sí*? You wake now.'

'What time is it?' Georgie sat up and sank back against the pillows as she watched the little maid draw back the drapes and let bright sunlight flood into the bedroom.

'Is ten o'clock, *señorita*.' And at Georgie's gasp of dismay, Pilar added, 'Is no problem. The *señor*, he have his swim an' he say for you to come to the breakfast, *sí*? In...' Pilar held up her fingers.

'Ten minutes?' Georgie suggested.

'*Sí, sí, señorita*. The ten minutes. Okay?'

'Okay.'

Once Pilar had left the room Georgie let the coffee cool a little while she had a quick shower, gulping it down as she partly blowdried her hair and then pulled it up in a loose ponytail on top of her head, although more strands fell about her face than stayed in the band.

She pulled on a pair of jeans and a skinny midnight-blue top and glanced at her watch. Ten minutes exactly. She'd better get downstairs.

She felt quite in control as she walked into the breakfast room but her aplomb was blown to pieces in the next moment. Matt was already sitting at the breakfast table casually reading a newspaper, and it was clear he had just showered, probably after his swim.

It was also clear he didn't believe in formal attire at the breakfast table. The black silk robe was open to the waist and the muscled hairy chest was the stuff dreams were made of. That, and the way his damp hair curled slightly over his forehead, softening the hard features and giving them a touch of dynamite, robbed Georgie of the power to respond immediately to his easy, 'Good morning.'

She lost the power to know how to walk as she tottered across the room towards the table, almost falling over her own feet, and by the time she sank gratefully into a chair her cheeks were scarlet.

'Did you sleep well?' Matt asked gravely, apparently not noticing he was sharing breakfast with a beetroot.

'Fine, thank you.' She cleared her throat twice. 'Have you rung the hospital yet? How's your mother?'

'She had a good night and my friend is with her now. He said they will operate first thing tomorrow, when he's had a chance to do some necessary tests.'

Georgie nodded in what she hoped was a calm, informed sort of way.

'Coffee?' He was already pouring her a cup as he spoke and the movement of the big male body sent her hormones spiralling.

'Thank you.' She took the cup from him and hurriedly gulped at it, burning the inside of her mouth and trying to pretend her eyes weren't watering with pain.

'Help yourself to cereal and fruit and croissants,' Matt said nonchalantly. 'Flora will be bringing in a cooked breakfast in a little while and she gets hurt if you don't clear the plate.'

'Does she?' Georgie was alarmed. She had seen the

amount of food Matt seemed able to tuck away with seemingly little effort, and the loaded tray Pillar had brought to her room when she had arrived the day before was in the forefront of her mind.

'I told her just a little for you,' Matt said soothingly. 'You don't eat much, do you?'

'I eat loads.' It was indignant. 'Don't forget I'm eight or nine inches smaller than you and probably weigh half as much. Women are built differently to men.'

It probably wasn't the cleverest thing she had ever said. She watched the dark eyes turn smoky as he murmured, 'I'm aware of that, Georgie.'

She dragged her eyes away from his face and the acres of bare flesh beneath it, and concentrated on the array of cereals, fruits, toast, croissants and preserves in the middle of the table, hastily reaching for a ripe peach and beginning to slice it on her plate. If she was having a cooked breakfast she wouldn't be able to manage anything more.

Matt demolished a bowl of muesli to which he added a sliced banana and peach, followed by two croissants heaped with blackcurrant preserve, before Flora appeared wheeling in the heated trolley holding their plates.

Georgie was eternally grateful that Flora had heeded Matt's advice where her plate was concerned, but she stared fascinated at the contents of Matt's plate.

'I'm a growing boy.' He had noticed her rapt contemplation and his voice was amused. 'I have to keep my strength up in hope of...'

'In hope of what?' she asked absently, her mind still occupied with the half a pound of sausages and bacon, three eggs, mushrooms, tomatoes, fried potatoes and onions adorning Matt's plate. And then, as the silence lengthened, she raised her eyes to his face and he said gravely, 'Just in hope.'

An image of that wickedly voluptuous bed flashed across her mind and she quickly lowered her eyes to her plate. He was too sexy and flagrantly male clothed, but partly clothed… She bit into a sausage and prayed for composure. What did he have on under that robe? A piece of mushroom went down the wrong way and she coughed and spluttered, her agitation not helped at all when Matt left his seat to come and pat her back and offer her a glass of water.

'I'm fine, really,' she mumbled, sniffing loudly and trying to ignore the muscled legs at the side of her. He could at least have put on some pyjama bottoms or something after his swim if he didn't want to get dressed, she told herself self-righteously. But perhaps he didn't wear pyjamas?

'Here.' He bent down, dabbing at her wet eyes with a napkin, and she caught the full impact of the smell of expensive body shampoo on clean male skin before he strolled round the table again.

She finished her breakfast without further mishap but with every nerve and muscle in her body as taut as piano wire and conscious of the slightest movement from the big male body opposite. Matt, on the other hand, appeared supremely relaxed, enjoying a leisurely breakfast with obvious enjoyment.

As well he might, Georgie thought feverishly. *She* wasn't the one flaunting herself! Although, to be fair, Matt didn't appear to be aware he was flaunting himself, she admitted silently. He was a man who was very much at ease with his own body, as his comment the day before about his preference for swimming and exercising in the nude proved. She didn't dare dwell on that thought.

'So…'

She raised her eyes as she forked the last mouthful of

food from the plate into her mouth, and saw Matt was looking at her with unfathomable eyes. 'Yes?' she asked warily.

'We will visit the hospital this afternoon after an early lunch,' Matt said decisively. 'What would you like to do this morning?'

The aggressive sexuality that was as frightening as it was exciting made her voice slightly shaky as she said, 'Anything, I don't mind.'

'If only...' He gave a small laugh, low in his throat, at her expression. 'Well, as it is no good my suggesting a lazy morning in bed, and you did your exploring of the gardens yesterday, perhaps it would be good to show you a little of the surrounding area, yes? And we can maybe stop for something to eat close to the hospital rather than come back here.'

'Whatever you think.'

'How submissive.'

She stared at him, not sure if he was being nasty or not, and suddenly his expression cleared and he smiled ruefully. 'There is something of the spoilt brat in every man, *pequeña*, and I have found since I met you I am like every man. I do not like this; I had thought myself above such ignoble behaviour, but it would seem you bring out the worst in me. Of course, if we were lovers all this tension would be dealt with and life would be sweeter for both of us.'

'Life is quite sweet enough, thanks,' she said tartly.

'Liar.' It was slightly taunting but said with a smile which Georgie found it difficult to return. He was such a *disturbing* man, she told herself resentfully. The last weeks she had felt she was living on a knife's edge all the time, and it was exhausting. The very air seemed to crackle with electricity when Matt was about and these moments of honesty he seemed to indulge in made things worse.

'Come.' He rose from the table, holding out his hand as

he walked round to her chair. 'If you feel the need to persist in this ridiculous wish to deny us both I can only be patient until you accept the error of your ways.'

'Matt—' Her voice was cut off as he pulled her to her feet and his mouth caught hers with an urgency that was thrilling. He kissed her long and deeply, draining her of sweetness before his lips moved to her ears and throat causing convulsive shivers of ecstasy.

Her fingertips slipped under the silk at his shoulders, roaming over the leanly muscled flesh beneath the robe before they tangled in the pleasing roughness of the hair on his broad chest and then up again to his hard neck.

He was all male and unbelievable sexy, and Georgie allowed herself another moment or two of heaven before she pulled firmly away.

'I know, you are not that sort of girl,' he murmured, not quite letting go of her as he looked down with smouldering eyes.

'What sort?' she asked with a trembling attempt at lightness.

'The sort who makes love on the floor of the breakfast room.'

If he loved her as she loved him it could be the breakfast room table and she wouldn't care! 'I think Pilar might be just a little surprised,' she managed fairly blandly. 'Don't you?' She removed herself from his hold, stepping back a pace as she said evenly, 'What time do you want to leave?'

'Half an hour?' he suggested softly. 'It will give me time to take a shower.'

'I though you had showered,' she said, surprised.

'A cold shower, Georgie.'

When Georgie stepped outside into the scented warmth of a hot Spanish day half an hour later, Matt was waiting for her. He was sitting at the wheel of a Mercedes-Benz SL convertible and the beautiful silver car purred gently to life as she slid into the passenger seat. 'Another boy's toy?' she asked lightly, partly to hide what the sight of him—clothed in black shirt and trousers—had done to her equilibrium.

'Just so.' He smiled, his teeth flashing white in the tanned skin of his face.

She enjoyed seeing more of the country of his birth nearly as much as she enjoyed being with him. They ate lunch in a shadow-blotched plaza in a small cobbled town, the tall tower of a brown church in the distance with a great bell outlined against the blue sky. It was heaven. Or, rather, being with Matt was heaven. And dangerous. And perilous. And a hundred other adjectives that described jeopardy.

When they arrived at the hospital Georgie found she was nervous. Excruciatingly nervous. Matt's mother was his nearest and dearest and although he had never said so in so many words she knew he loved his mother deeply. And his mother was a friend of Pepita's.

The hospital was luxurious, and obviously not run of the mill, and Matt seemed to be something of an icon. They were practically bowed along the thickly carpeted corridor to his mother's room, although the sister in charge left them at the door at Matt's quietly polite request.

'Just be yourself.' She wasn't sure if he had sensed her agitation but his voice was distinctly soothing. 'You'll get on like a house on fire.'

No pressure! But before she could say a word he had knocked and opened the door, his voice warm as he said, 'Visitors for Señora de Capistrano?'

'Matt...' The voice was English but perfumed with a melodious sweetness that suggested years in a warm climate as it said, 'I have been waiting for you and Georgie.'

Georgie wasn't aware she had been ushered into the room; all her senses were tied up with Matt's mother.

Señora de Capistrano was one of those women whose age was immaterial compared to her beauty. She must have been over fifty—Matt was thirty-six after all—but the blonde-haired woman lying in the bed could have been any age from forty upwards. Her blonde hair was threaded with silver, which only seemed to add a luminescence to her faintly lined, creamy skin, and her blue eyes were of a deep violet shade that was truly riveting.

She was beautiful, outstandingly beautiful, and she was smiling a sweet, warm smile that took Georgie completely by surprise. She didn't know what she had been expecting—perhaps a strong reserve, even hostility in view of the fact that Pepita was a friend—but Matt's mother was either an incredible actress or genuinely pleased to see her.

'Georgie, this is my mother.' Matt's voice was tender. 'Mother, Georgie.'

'Come and sit down, dear.' One pale slim hand indicated the chair at the side of the bed, and as Matt went to draw another from across the room his mother said quickly, 'I understand the doctor, your friend Jeff Eddleston, wants a word, dear. He was most insistent you see him as soon as you arrived. I think he wants to go to his hotel and go to bed as soon as he can.' The violet gaze included Georgie as Matt's mother said, her voice indulgent now, 'My son summoned poor Mr Eddleston from halfway across the world in the middle of the night, and he came. That is true friendship, don't you think?'

Georgie was of the opinion that Matt could summon almost anyone without a refusal—he was that sort of man—but she simply smiled and left it at that.

'Now?' Matt was clearly loath to leave.

'Now.' Señora de Capistrano smiled gently. 'He's a brilliant doctor, so I understand? Everyone is in awe of him here.'

Matt's expression said very clearly that he was not. 'I won't be long.'

'Take all the time you need, dear. Georgie and I will get to know each other a little.'

When the door had closed behind her son, Señor de Capistrano turned her violet gaze on Georgie and looked at her for a long moment. 'So you are the one,' she said softly.

'I'm sorry?' Georgie stared at her bewilderly.

'Matt has spoken of his English ''friend'' more than once lately, but I did not think it would be in these surroundings that we met.' It was a touch rueful.

'You're feeling a bit better, I understand?' Georgie said carefully.

'Yes, yes.' It was impatient, and for the first time Georgie could see Matt in the beautiful woman in front of her. There was a moment's pause, and then Matt's mother said, 'My name is Julia, Georgie. I would like us to be friends.'

'So would I.' Georgie was out of her depth and it showed.

'Can I talk to you confidentially?' The lovely eyes were piercing. 'You know I am to have an operation tomorrow?' Georgie nodded. 'Then I am claiming that as my reason for putting aside all politeness and convention and coming straight to the kernel in the nut,' Julia continued urgently. 'I love my son, Georgie. I want the very best for him; he deserves it.'

It could have been unfriendly but it wasn't, neither was it inimical. Georgie sat and waited, knowing it was a time to be silent.

'When I met my husband and we fell in love there was

great opposition from his family.' It wasn't what Georgie had expected to hear and her eyes opened wide for a moment, but Julia continued, 'We weathered the storm until we came into calmer waters, and that only happened after Matthew was born. I was accepted then. I had given my husband a son so all was well, and it didn't matter I was English. As far as Matthew's father and I were concerned it hadn't mattered anyway. We loved each other, deeply. If we had been childless all our lives we would still have been together, loving each other.'

'You were very fortunate,' Georgie said softly. 'My brother and his wife were like that.'

The silver-blonde head nodded in acknowledgement. 'Matthew was brought up in a loving home,' Julia said quietly, 'but he also has the genes from his father's people in his blood. My husband was a wonderful man, kind and gentle, but not so his parents or their parents. They were very proud and hard, one could say cruel even.'

'I don't understand?' Georgie said quietly.

'They were the kind of people who never forgot an insult or a harm done to them,' Julia said softly. 'Vendettas, blood feuds, honour. This was the language they talked and lived. My son is not like his father, Georgie, but neither is he all his grandparents either. There is a little of both in my Matt, I think, and life will shape which takes pre-eminence. Life...or a woman.'

Georgie looked at the woman in front of her, her eyes wide with sudden understanding. But Julia had got it all wrong, she thought feverishly. Matt didn't love her; she had no sway over him except that he wanted her body for a brief time. But how could she say that to his mother?

'When such a person as my son is hurt or betrayed it goes deep.' Julia was no longer looking at Georgie but had turned to gaze out of the big picture window opposite the bed, where the tops of green trees could be seen beneath a cloudless blue sky. 'And it takes an equally deep feeling to cauterise the pain and bring about healing.'

'Julia?' Georgie didn't know what to say but she had to say something to stop this terrible misunderstanding. 'If you are saying what I think you're saying, that I am the one to bring about the healing from some incident in Matt's past, you've got it all wrong. He doesn't love me; he has already told me he doesn't believe in love or commitment.'

'Honour and pride.' It was said on a sigh.

She had to say it, crass though it might sound. Georgie took a deep breath and said quietly, 'He wants an affair, that's all. A brief interlude. He…he is interested because I haven't immediately fallen into bed with him.'

Julia's amazing eyes fastened on Georgie's flushed face, and they stayed there for what seemed like an endless time. And then Matt's mother said quietly, 'He needs you, Georgie, but how do you feel? Do you care for him? Really care for him?'

It took more strength than Julia was aware of for Georgie to strip off the armour and say steadily, 'Yes, I do, but I'd prefer him not to know.'

'I can understand that, and I promise you he will not learn it from me. But in return for that confidence I want to tell you something. Something very private and something I have not spoken of before, not to anyone. But you, you I want to tell.'

Georgie stared into the beautiful face and she felt a shiver run down her spine. This had been far from a cosy chat and she had the feeling it was about to get worse.

'When Matthew went to university he was a bright, strong boy with a zest for life that was unquenchable and a warmth that was very much like his father's,' Julia began slowly. 'When he graduated the brightness and strength was still there, but the zest for life had been turned into a desire to take it by the throat and the warmth was quite gone. This...' Julia hesitated, her hand moving to her throat. 'This was due to a girl.'

'Begonia.'

'He has spoken to you of Begonia?' It was sharp and Julia's face was amazed.

'No. Well, yes. At least...' Georgie tried to pull her thoughts together. 'He said he knew her for eighteen months and then it finished,' she said quickly.

Julia looked at her for another moment before nodding. 'It is not as simple as that, but then knowing my son you would not have expected it to be. He was in love with Begonia and she betrayed him,' she said flatly. 'But not in the normal sense. They were together for a year—you know?'

Georgie nodded painfully. Yes, she knew.

'And then something dreadful happened. We received a phone call from the university to say that Matt was missing and that the police were involved. Then came a ransom note. It stated Matt was being held until we delivered a certain amount of money to a designated pick-up point. We delivered. Matt was released from the tiny underground room he had been held in for five days and left in the middle of nowhere. But my son is no fool, Georgie.

'He had taken a note of sounds and driving distances, even though he was blindfolded and cuffed, and eventually the police found the street and then the actual cellar. Then it got worse. I won't bore you with the details, but suffice to say he had been held by supposed friends who needed money for their drug addiction.'

The claustrophobia. Georgie stared at Matt's mother in horror. 'Begonia was one of them?' she whispered weakly.

Julia nodded. 'Matt did not know about her drug habit;

perhaps he would have helped her if he did. Anyway, needless to say, the abduction affected him deeply. He...he was not the same afterwards. He became very cynical and cold.'

Georgie nodded. She could understand that. 'And Begonia?' she asked quietly.

'Begonia and the others received a severe prison sentence. The parents of one of the boys involved got a clever lawyer, who insisted it was just an ill-advised practical joke which had gone wrong, but in view of the sum of money involved this argument was not acceptable. It transpired Begonia had been sharing her favours with this boy as well as Matt.'

Georgie shook her head slowly, her hair brushing her cheeks in a shimmering veil. For a first love to go wrong was bad enough, but in those circumstances...

'Matt has had women companions since then, of course, but he has chosen only those who were beautiful enough and shallow enough to fit into his lifestyle. Francisca calls them dolls and she is right. Matt only smiles when his sister says this, but when he spoke of you... He did not smile. No, he did not smile.'

'Julia—' Georgie squirmed on the upholstered seat. 'He doesn't *love* me. Whatever he feels, he's made it clear it's not love.'

'Then he is a fool,' Matt's mother said very softly, her eyes gentle on the lovely face in front of her.

'That's what Matt called Glen,' Georgie said ruefully. 'My ex. He...he let me down rather badly.'

'And Matt called him a fool? Well, well.' Julia lay back against the plump pillows behind her and surveyed Georgie afresh. 'Don't give up on him, Georgie. Not yet. It takes time to climb out of the darkness into the light, especially when that darkness is the only protection you have against a giant step that makes Neil Armstrong's look easy. I know my son. I know what is of his father. My husband loved me utterly and absolutely, and that is the way Matt will love when he finds the right woman.'

And if she wasn't the right woman? Where did that leave her? Georgie's green eyes were cloudy. Matt's mother loved him and that was right and proper, but it coloured her viewpoint to look at things for Matt's good. What about *her* good?

Matt could have any woman he wanted and he couldn't fail to recognise the fact by the number which pursued him. He was handsome and wealthy and powerful, and she was an ordinary girl from a little town in England he had happened to meet, and who didn't tell him exactly what he wanted to hear. That had interested him, intrigued him even. But what happened when the chase stopped and the hunter got his quarry?

'I think you're mistaken about me,' Georgie said quietly, 'about how Matt feels, but thank you for telling me about what happened in his past anyway. It…it explains a lot.'

Julia nodded. 'It does, doesn't it?' she agreed softly. 'But as to my being mistaken… Well, time will tell, Georgie.'

Time. Would it be friend or foe? She wished she could believe for the former but cold reason told her it would be the latter.

And then the door opened and Matt was back, and in spite of all her fears Georgie's heart leapt as she looked at him.

They spent over an hour at the hospital and by the time they left Georgie knew she could love Matt's mother. Julia was so sweet, so warm; she could understand what had attracted Matt's father to his English bride after being brought up in a home which, by the sound of it, although palatial, had been devoid of much love and laughter.

'You'll come again before you leave?' As Georgie made her goodbyes, Julia's voice was insistent.

'If you want me to.'

'I do.'

It was very definite, and once outside in the corridor Matt took her arm, drawing her round to face him as he said softly, 'I told you you two would like each other.'

And it was ridiculous, really ridiculous, and probably just because her emotions had been oversensitised during the talk with Julia, but somehow Georgie got the strangest feeling he wasn't altogether pleased at how things had gone. The grey eyes looked down at her, their expression hidden behind congeniality, and then they were walking down the corridor again and the moment was lost as they enjoyed the rest of the day together.

Julia's operation went well the next morning, and after Matt had visited the hospital he returned before lunch and found Georgie in the gardens, his voice light and easy as he said, 'Grab a swimming costume and a towel, I'm taking you to a beach I know where we can swim and laze the afternoon away.'

'But lunch?'

'Flora's packing a picnic hamper,' he said smoothly. 'We'll eat on the way; I know a spot, and I prefer it to having sand in my food.'

She nodded, but her smile was faintly wary. He had been different since their visit to see his mother the day before. The rest of the afternoon and evening spent sightseeing had been lovely, and the small restaurant at which they had eaten—surrounded by fragrant almond groves—had been magical, but there had been a distance, a coolness in Matt she was sure she hadn't imagined. Or maybe she had. She didn't know where she was when she was within six feet of him!

She had had the foresight to bring her own swimming costume with her from England—a somewhat uninteresting one-piece in dark blue so after picking up a bath towel from her bathroom Georgie joined Matt on the drive outside where he was just putting the picnic basket into the car.

He surveyed her slim shape clothed in three-quarter length jeans and a figure-hugging top in bright poppy-red silently for a moment, before he said quietly, 'Youth personified.'

'Hardly.' Georgie pushed back a strand of silky hair, tucking it behind her ear, as she said, 'I am twenty-three, Matt.'

'Ancient,' he agreed drily.

She stared at him, uncertain of his mood but knowing there was something she didn't like in his tone, and then slid into the car silently. If he wanted an argument he could argue with himself; she only had a few days here with him and they were going to have to provide a lifetime of memories.

Once they were on their way, however, the brief unease was lulled by the ever-changing vista outside the car. Sugar-white houses with balconies of iron covered in morning glory, flowered walled gardens adjoining small orchards, simple granite churches and quiet lanes hedged with hibiscus and jacaranda—Georgie drank in the rich tapestry of views and scents and began to relax.

She had vowed she would live life minute by minute with Matt, expecting nothing, and she wasn't going to spoil today by thinking too much, she decided, just after the car passed two small bare-footed children. The tiny tots were leading a bewhiskered nanny goat along the dusty road by means of a piece of frayed rope tied round its furry neck.

She had to stop examining everything his mother had said, she told herself firmly, and hoping for a miracle.

'Here.' Beyond the small village they had just passed stretched green meadows, and now Matt turned the car off the road and on to an unmade track winding away into the distance. 'I know the perfect spot for a picnic.'

After some two hundred yards or so he stopped the car. 'Look over there,' he said quietly. 'My mother and father used to bring Francisca and myself here before we went on to the beach, and my sister liked it better than the sea. She was frightened of the waves, you see, but this was safe to paddle in.'

Georgie looked. The grass sloped down to a small, crystal-clear stream fringed with pebbles, the water running with gurgling purpose over smooth mounds of polished rock. It was an enchanting little dell and she could just imagine the delight of two small children eating a picnic by the side of the stream.

Had he brought other women to this idyllic haven of days gone by? Days when he had been carefree and happy? She didn't dare ask. Instead she said, her voice very even, 'Does Francisca bring her children here?'

'That tribe of monkeys?' Dark eyes crinkled as he smiled and Georgie's heart was rent with love. 'She would never round them all up again if she let them loose in the open.'

'I'm sure they're not as bad as all that?' Georgie said reprovingly.

'Worse than you could imagine,' he returned drily as he opened his car door, walking round the bonnet and helping her to alight before he reached for the picnic basket and blanket in the back of the car. 'If I ever needed anything to convince me that marriage and children and settling down is not for me, a visit to my sister's house would do it. Bedlam. All the time.'

It was too softly vehement. Georgie watched him as he carried the hamper down to the stream, but it was some moments before she moved herself. If that hadn't been a warning, or at least a reminder, of all he had said in the past she didn't know what was! How dared he? How *dared* he warn her off like that? And then a terrible thought struck—had his mother told him what she had admitted yesterday, that she loved him? But no, no, she trusted Julia. This was just Matt being Matt.

Her stomach was churning as she sat down on the blanket he had spread out on the grass, but his remark had brought her up with a jolt. Which was probably exactly what she had needed, she admitted ruefully.

The picnic was definitely a de Capistrano one, and therefore in a different league from anything masquerading under that name which Georgie had enjoyed in the past. Wine, Flora's delicious home-made lemonade, slices of ham, turkey, beef and pork, crusty bread and little pats of butter, ripe red tomatoes, crisp salad, hard-boiled eggs, pâté, little savoury pastries, tiny tubs of fondant potatoes, goat's cheese, olives; the list went on and on, and that was before they looked at the various individual portions of mouth-watering desserts Flora had included.

'How many people did Flora think were coming on this picnic?' Georgie asked after they had eaten hungrily in companionable silence for some minutes.

'Just you and I, *pequeña*.' Matt had had one glass of the fruity red wine Flora had included before refilling his glass with lemonade, but now he poured more of the rich blackcurranty liquid into her glass before lying back on the blanket and shutting his eyes against the glare of the sun.

Georgie looked at him at the side of her, the big lean body stretched out like a relaxed panther but with all the inherent dangerousness of the big cat merely harnessed for the moment. A small pulse was beating at the base of his tanned throat and she had an overwhelming urge to place her lips to it before she took hold of herself firmly.

Matt had perfect control of his emotions. Why couldn't she feel the same? She drank the wine in a few hasty gulps, the warmth of it comforting after the bleakness of her thoughts, and then lay back on the sunwarmed blanket herself. He could pick her up or put her down seemingly just as he pleased whereas her head, her mind, her soul were all filled with him twenty-four hours a day. But then her heart was involved, not just her body. Unlike his.

The sun was warm on her face, a gentle breeze caressing her skin idly as it wafted the scent of a hundred wild flowers against the background music of the gurgling water. She must have slept, because when she became aware of the mouth brushing her lips it seemed part of the dream she had been having. An erotic, disturbing dream.

She opened dazed green eyes and looked into Matt's face above her and for a long moment they were both immobile, drowning in each other's eyes. Then with a muffled sound which came deep from his throat he pulled her into him, turning so that she was lying across his hard chest, her racing pulse echoing the slam of his heart.

The kiss was achingly sweet, his mouth pleasuring them both as it explored hers. A deep languorous warmth was filling her, moving into every little crevice and nerve and causing her body to throb as the ache inside her slowly ripened.

And then he lifted her from him, his voice none too steady as he said, 'Time to go, I think, or we will never have that swim.'

She didn't care about that, about the beach! She just wanted to stay here for ever, in this little place away from the real world and reality. She watched him sit up, his back tense under the black cloth of his shirt, but when he turned to face her he was composed again, the lover of a few moments ago gone.

'It is not far.' He offered her his hand as he rose to his feet and she accepted it with a smile that was forced. 'And the sea is perfect today, calm and tranquil.'

Unlike her! Georgie shut her eyes for a second as he gathered the hamper together, and then opened them to watch him pack the basket with expert precision. But then he did everything perfectly, she thought with a moment's bitterness. That was the trouble.

It was just after three o'clock and the sun was high when Matt drove the car out of the long winding lane they had been following for the last five minutes, and out on to the tough springy grass beyond which stretched the sort of beach Georgie had only seen in advertisements on the TV.

The secluded bay was set against a dramatic backdrop of pine-clad hills and in the far distance blue-mauve mountains. The dazzling white beach was strewn with delicate rose-pink and mother-of-pearl shells beyond which lapped vivid turquoise-blue water.

Matt had stopped the car and Georgie was aware of him watching her face, but it was some moments before she could drag her eyes away from the enchantment in front of her and say softly, 'It's the most beautiful place in the world, Matt. Thank you for showing it to me.'

Something worked in his face as she spoke but his voice was restrained when he said, 'My pleasure, Miss Millett.'

'Matt—' She stopped abruptly, not knowing how to continue but conscious of his pain beneath the composed mask he wore. There had been something in his expression, almost an acceptance, that had sent a chill flickering down her spine. His will was iron-like, the intensity of the spirit deep inside the man frightening. She could never reach him, never get through to the hurt individual behind the mask. She just didn't know *how*.

'Yes?'

'It doesn't matter.'

By the time Georgie had struggled into her swimming costume under the towel Matt was already in the clear blue water, and he waved to her from where he was swimming in the slight swell of the waves.

The sand was hot beneath her feet as she ran down to the water's edge, but at least she felt *herself* in her own swimming costume, she told herself bracingly.

In spite of the warmth of the sun the water was icy cold, and she gasped as she waded further and further towards Matt, although once she was swimming she didn't notice the cold any more. The water was silky, wonderful, and the small turquoise waves were totally non-threatening.

She lost sight of Matt just when she thought she was close to him, and then squealed in surprise—taking in a mouthful of salt water in the process—as he emerged just in front of her like a genie from the depths of a bottle.

'You did that on purpose!' she glared at him, but then, as he gathered her to him and kissed her thoroughly, the pair of them sinking under the clear water, she forgot to be angry. This was paradise; it was, it was paradise, and she would never feel so alive, so *aware* in the whole of her life.

They spent a crazy half-hour in the water, acting like two kids let out of school for the day, before Georgie, utterly exhausted, made for the shore. Matt had indicated he wanted to do some serious swimming before he came in, and after she had collapsed on the blanket he had brought from the car Georgie watched him for a few minutes.

The hard lean body cut through the water with military

precision, and she found herself wondering at the ruthless determination which drove him to push himself to the limit. Most people found swimming therapeutic, but she had the idea that to Matt it was just another area in which he had to prove to himself he could do it alone—beat the elements. It saddened her, taking some of the joy out of the time they had shared, and she lay back on the blanket, suddenly weary.

The air was warm and salty, the lapping of the tiny waves on the beach a soothing background music, but she couldn't really relax. After a little while she became aware the sun was too hot to ignore and sat up, wrapping the towel round her cocoon-fashion as she continued to watch Matt in the water.

And then he came out. He might just as well have been nude for all the tiny black briefs concealed.

Georgie watched, fascinated, as the lithe, tanned body strolled up the beach towards her. The hair on his powerful chest narrowed to a thin line bisecting his flat belly, and the smooth-muscled hips and long strong legs were magnificent. *He* was magnificent, every perfectly honed inch of him.

She couldn't tear her eyes away from him as he came nearer, even though she knew he must be aware she was ogling him, and it was only when he was within a few yards of her that she found the strength to lower her eyes and pretend to fiddle with the towel.

'Enjoy yourself?'

'What?' For an awful minute Georgie thought he was referring to her brazen gawping.

'The sea is so much better than even the best swimming pool, don't you think?' he said.

She forced herself to say, 'Definitely. Oh, definitely.'

'Fancy a drink?'

'What?' Oh, she had to stop saying that, she thought a trifle desperately.

'A drink?' he reiterated patiently. 'I'll bring the picnic basket down.'

'Great.'

Great, great, great! Please put some clothes on! She watched him pad towards the car and she watched him return, and she wondered if he was aware of how woefully inadequate the small piece of cloth round his hips was. But if he was, he didn't care. She shut her eyes tightly for a second as he threw himself down beside her on the blanket, and then opened them wide when he said coolly, 'Wine or lemonade?'

She didn't need anything to heat her blood further! 'Lemonade, please.'

He poured her a glass, and then himself, downing his in a few swallows before lying back on the blanket contentedly. 'This is very good.'

Speak for yourself. 'Yes, it's very nice,' she said faintly. 'Few people know of this bay; it is usually deserted.'

That wasn't actually much comfort right at this moment. She glanced at him warily. 'You must be exhausted after all that swimming,' she said carefully. 'You were in the water for more than an hour.'

'No, I am not tired, Georgie.'

She knew what was coming. She had known from the moment they had walked on to this beach what he had in mind, but as he rolled over and took her into his arms she made no attempt to push him away. She wanted him. The rights and wrongs of it suddenly didn't matter any more. She needed him in a way she had never imagined she could need anyone.

His lips were first coaxingly seductive, and then, when she met his kiss for kiss, fiercely erotic. He penetrated the softness of her mouth with his tongue, producing flickers of sensual awareness from the tips of her toes to the top of her head, his increasingly urgent caresses reflecting the fine tremors shivering across his muscled body.

'You taste and feel so good,' he murmured huskily. 'Deliciously salty-sweet and incredibly soft. Hell, Georgie, do you know what you do to me?'

The question was rhetorical, the leashed power of his arousal all too evident. It brought a fiercely primitive response from the depths of her, a wild satisfaction that his body couldn't deny his need of her. She could feel his shudders of pleasure and she exulted in them, in his strength, his maleness.

She loved him. She wanted to know what it would be like to make love with him. It was as simple as that in the end.

His hands were moving over the silky soft material of her swimsuit with slow, tantalising sureness, causing her body to spring to life beneath his fingers. Her nipples were erect and hard under their cover, her whole being gripped by quivering sexual tension.

She opened her eyes, which had been shut, so she could see his face, and his eyes looked back at her, hot and dark and glittering. But he wasn't rushing her. She was aware of this. His hands and mouth were moving with seductive insistence and creating rivulets of fire wherever they touched and teased, but this was no swift animal mating but rather one of calculated finesse. He was making her liquid with desire and he knew it; knew every single response he drew forth before she did.

She was responding to his expert mastery with instinctive passion and desire born of her love for him, and just for a moment she felt a vague sense of loss that it wasn't that way for him. He wasn't being swept along by love for her, he merely wanted her. It was just sex for him. But then he moved in a certain way, his hard chest creating a tight, exquisite pressure over her aching breasts and she forgot to think, forgot everything in the sensation after sensation washing over her body.

'Georgie, say it. Say you want me.' He was murmuring against her hot skin, his voice a low growl. 'Say you want me like I want you.'

He raised himself slightly, looking down into her dazed face as his hands cupped her cheeks.

'Say you want me to undress you, to take you here on the sands with the sky above us. Tell me.'

She stared up at him with drowning green eyes, gasping slightly as his hands moved to her breasts, shaping their full roundness through the fabric of her swimming costume. And she said the only words that were in her heart, 'I love you, so much,' as her head moved from side to side in a feverish agony of need, her eyes closing.

'No, say it as it is. No pretence, Georgie, not between us.'

For a moment she didn't understand, lost as she was in a spinning world of sensation and light, and then as his fingers traced a path into the soft hollow of her breasts before he began to peel the swimming costume away she understood what he was demanding. This had to be on his terms; he wanted her to tell him she was inviting him into her body, that she wanted and needed him, but she wasn't allowed to say love. *But she did love him.*

'I love you.' This time it wasn't said with frenzied desire but was a statement of fact, and Matt recognised it as such, his hands freezing on her body.

She lay very still, looking up at him, allowing him to see the truth in her eyes, and as she saw the shock on his face slowly being absorbed by the coldness spreading over it she knew she would remember this moment all of her life.

'No, no, you do not.'

'Yes, I do.' As his hands left her she sat up quickly, adjusting the swimming costume and drawing the towel round her shoulders. Suddenly, in spite of the heat of the sun, she felt cold. 'You might not like it,' she said with painful dignity as he sat, half turned away from her, his profile hard and stunned, 'but nevertheless that's how it is. You asked for no pretence between us, Matt, after all. And you might as well know the rest of it now. I wanted to make love with you *because* I love you, and there has never been anyone else in that way.'

'You're telling me you didn't sleep with Glen?' Although his voice was very flat she sensed the shock.

'No, I didn't. It just didn't seem right, somehow, but until I met you I hadn't realised why. But I didn't love him, not as you're supposed to love the person you want to be with for the rest of your life.' There, she'd said it. It would do no good, she knew that, but she couldn't have gone the rest of the life wondering whether if he knew it would have touched something deep inside. It was scant comfort when she looked at his rigid face, but at least he had heard it as it really was. The ball was well and truly in his court.

'I never made you any promises, Georgie.' His voice was cold now, his accent strong, and he still didn't look at her. 'You knew how it was all along, how I feel about the sort of commitment you are talking about. I am not cut out for togetherness; I do not want it.'

'Why are you so frightened to say the word?' she asked quietly. 'Because love goes hand in hand with the possibility of betrayal and loss?'

He did look at her then, his grey eyes as sharp as cut slate.

'This Begonia you told me about, the girl at university, she hurt you badly, didn't she?' His mother had said she'd never talked about it to anyone and Georgie had the feeling Matt hadn't, either. 'What happened, Matt?' she prompted softly, hoping her voice didn't betray the way she was shaking inside with the enormity of the confrontation. If he would just tell her, open up a little...

He drew in a deep hard breath. 'It will accomplish nothing to talk about it,' he said gratingly. 'The past is the past.'

'But it isn't the past for you, not really,' she countered steadily. 'And until it is you'll never be able to reach out for the future.'

'Save me the trite platitudes, Georgie!'

'You want to row with me, don't you?' she said, struggling for composure in the face of his anger. 'Attack is the best defence and all that. And it's just to cover up the fact that you are scared stiff to take a chance and trust someone!'

'You want to hear about Begonia?' he rasped bitterly. 'Then I will tell you! Every little sordid detail.' And he did. He told her it all, his voice sinisterly quiet now and very cold.

Georgie stared at him the whole time. He was right; this had accomplished nothing, she realised miserably, except to make him hate her. She had expected he would feel some relief in the telling, but instead, in revealing what he saw as his humiliation and defeat, she had made him hate her. He was a proud man, obsessionally so. He would never forgive her for this.

'She was sick, Matt.' When he had finished talking and the silence became painful Georgie's voice was a whisper. 'Sick in mind and body, and someone like that can't love anything or anyone. Love is not like that—'

'And what makes you the expert?' As he swung to face her again his voice was savage.

'How I feel about you.'

He flinched visibly, but almost immediately rose to his feet, his face icy-cold. 'You are talking about sexual attraction,' he said stonily, 'although you have dressed it up to appear as something else to placate the conscience years and years of civilisation has bred. You are fooling yourself, Georgie. The emotion you are talking about does not exist in the pure form. A biological urge to mate, a wish for a nest and procreation, a need for protection or warmth, security—all those are facets of this thing you call love. It is totally unnatural to expect two people to live together for the rest of their lives. Man is not a monogamous animal.'

She had lost him. Or perhaps you had to have something in the first place to lose it, and she had never had Matt. 'I don't believe that and I don't think you do, not in your deepest heart of hearts.' Her voice *was* shaking now, she could hear it. 'There *is* a kind of love that lasts for ever, a kind that wants and needs intimacy and commitment and all that embraces. My brother and his wife had it, and I think your parents did too.'

'You know nothing about my parents,' he said cuttingly, 'so do not presume to lecture me.'

She had stood to her feet as he had been talking, and now her head jerked back as his arrogance hit a nerve. For the first time since they had been talking raw anger flooded her and she didn't try to quench it. She needed its fortifying heat to combat the agony inside. 'Lecture you?' she said with acidic mockery. 'Lecture *you*, the great Matt de Capistrano? I wouldn't dare! How could a mere mortal like me dare to disagree or venture a opinion in such exalted presence?'

'Do not be childish.'

'I might be childish but I'd rather be that than a block of stone like you,' she shot back furiously, his coldness serving to inflame her more. 'At least I'm alive, Matt! I feel, I ache, I cry—I do all the normal things that human beings do. Sure, life can make us wish we'd never been born on occasion, but real people fight back. You have let Begonia destroy you, do you realise that? They might have released you from that hole in the ground but you've dug yourself a deeper and more terrible one. You're not a man; you're a dead thing.'

'Have you quite finished?' It was thunderous.

'Oh, yes, I've finished all right. With you, with this ridiculous farce, with this country! I want to go home.' The last five words came out in a wail which wasn't at all the impression she wanted to give after he'd labelled her childish.

'I promise you you will be on the first available flight to England tomorrow,' he bit out caustically.

'Careful, Matt.' She might be devastated but he wasn't going to crush her completely! 'Promises aren't your thing.'

The drive home was the sort of nightmare Georgie wouldn't have inflicted on her worst enemy.

Matt's face could have been cut in stone and he didn't look at her or speak to her once. Georgie sat, huddled on her seat with her side pressed up against the car, as her mind reiterated all the harsh words she had thrown at him. And they had been harsh, she told herself with utter misery. She loved him, she loved him with all her heart, and all she had done was to call him names. She should have been understanding, kind, loving, showed him that true love turned the other cheek and that it didn't matter to her how he was, she still adored him.

But he was so arrogant, so infuriating, so altogether impossible! She had never even considered she'd got a temper before she'd met Matt, and then, boy, had it come to the fore! But all she'd said... She shut her eyes tightly and then opened them again, staring blankly through the windscreen without seeing a thing. She dared bet no one had ever spoken to him like that in his life. How could he make her say things like that when she loved him so much? She'd give the world to be able to heal the wounds Begonia and his so-called friends had inflicted.

When they drew up outside the house Matt left the car and opened her door—courteous to the last, Georgie thought with agonising black humour—but he didn't say a word until they were standing in the hall. 'You must be tired after such an exhausting day,' he bit out tightly, his grey eyes granite-hard as they looked down at her. 'I will see that Flora sends a tray up to your room after you have bathed and got ready for bed.'

In other words he didn't want to see her again until she left for England tomorrow. Georgie nodded stiffly, raising her small chin and calling on every scrap of tattered dignity she had left as she said, 'Thank you, but I am not hungry.'

'Nevertheless a tray will be brought to you.'

Do what you want; you always do anyway. She inclined her head before turning away and walking towards the staircase on legs that trembled. He was an unfeeling monster, that was what he was.

Once in her bedroom Georgie sat on the bed for long minutes before she could persuade her legs to carry her into the bathroom.

She wanted to cry, needed the relief of tears, but deep inside there only seemed to be dry ashes, which was making her feel worse.

After a warm bath she washed her hair and pulled on her towelling robe, wandering out into the sitting room and walking on to the balcony where the scented twilight was heavy with the last rays of the sun. She lifted her face to the sultry air, hearing the birds twittering and calling as they began to settle down for the night, and wondered how she could still walk and talk when her heart had been torn out by its roots. But this was just the beginning; she was going to have to learn to deal with this pain for the rest of her life—a life without Matt.

Flora brought her the tray ten minutes later, but although she thanked Matt's housekeeper, and smiled fairly normally, she knew she wouldn't be able to eat a thing and didn't even bother to uncover the dishes, although she took the large glass of white wine the tray held out on to the balcony with her. She sat down in the cushioned wicker chair it held, sipping the wine as her eyes wandered over the magnificent view.

She didn't regret saying everything she'd said, not really, she decided after a long while. She just wished she'd said it differently, that was all. Not in anger.

The dusk was falling rapidly now, the sky pouring flaming rivulets of scarlet, gold and orange across its wide expanse of light-washed blue. It was beautiful, magnificent, but tonight its beauty didn't touch her soul with joy and that frightened her. She felt as dead inside as she had accused Matt of being, and something of this feeling was reflected in her voice when she heard Flora behind her.

'The tray's on the little table, Flora,' she said dully without turning round. 'I'm sorry I couldn't eat anything but I think I've probably had too much sun today.'

'Forgive me, Georgie.'

She heard the voice almost without it registering for a stunned moment, and then she shot round, spilling the wine and with her hand to her throat as she saw Matt just behind her.

He looked terrible, awful. And wonderful. Her heart gave a mighty jolt and began to race like a greyhound, and she knew she wasn't dead inside after all as the pain hit. 'What…what do you want?'

'For you to keep on loving me.' He made no attempt to come any nearer.

'You don't believe in love,' she said, her face awash with the tears she'd thought she couldn't cry.

'If what I feel for you isn't love, then all the poets have got it wrong,' he said with grating pain. 'From the first moment I saw you it was there, Georgie. I tried to tell myself it was a million other things—sexual attraction, desire—but you've heard all that. I…I can't let you leave me, Georgie. I will die if you leave me. I haven't recognised myself the last few weeks and it has terrified me.'

The last was said with a kind of angry bewilderment which would have been funny in any other circumstances.

'You…you wouldn't die. What about Pepita and all the others?' She hadn't realised until she had said the name how much the other woman's presence in his life still rankled.

'Pepita?' He made an irritable, disdainful movement with his hand, and the meaning behind it almost made Georgie feel sorry for the beautiful Spanish woman. Almost. 'Pepita is like a sister to me; I have told you this. And there are no others. There will never be any others now I have met you. You have done this; you have ruined me for anyone else.'

'You said…' Georgie took a great gulp of air, trying to control her quivering bottom lip. 'You said—'

'I know what I said.' His voice was a deep hard groan. 'I said you were fooling yourself, all the time knowing it was I who was in that state of mind, not you. You challenged me that I was frightened of speaking the word love because of all it entailed, and this is true. This was true.'

'So what's changed?' she asked, seeing him through a mist of tears. 'What's changed your mind?'

'The thought of losing you, my love.'

It was the endearment she had never thought to hear from him and Georgie found she couldn't take it in. 'You wanted an affair,' she accused tremulously.

'I still do. An affair that lasts the rest of our lives and beyond, a real love affair. I want *you*, Georgie. Not just a warm body in my bed. I want us to be everything to each other; wife and husband, lovers, friends, and, yes, I admit that still terrifies me, but not as much as living life without you. When you confessed your love for me today I knew this. You know the land I bought? Where the butterflies live?' he asked suddenly.

'The butterflies?' And then she caught her thoughts. 'Oh, yes, Newbottle Meadow.'

'It will not be built on,' he said softly. 'I have already purchased new land, an old factory site that is *very* ugly, and this will be Robert's new undertaking. I have informed the authorities that I will be turning the land into a wildlife sanctuary and a place for people to walk, and will be donating an annual sum for its upkeep and so on.'

'When did you do that?' she asked dazedly.

'When I met the girl I had been waiting for all my life,' he said simply. 'Weeks ago. It will be called "Georgie's Meadow" from now on.'

For a moment Georgie stared blankly at him. 'Me?' she said.

'You.' And now he took her in his arms, kissing her long and hard until she was breathless. 'My love, for ever.'

'I want babies,' she warned ecstatically, wondering how a kiss could wipe away all the agony of the last hours.

'So do I, *pequeña*, hundreds.'

'They might be like Francisca's children!'

'They will be perfect. How could they be anything else when they have a perfect mother?' he said tenderly, picking her up as though she weighed nothing at all and sitting down with her in the chair, before kissing her again until she was weak and trembling in his arms.

'Matt?' When she finally managed to pull away to look at him, her eyes were bright and her mouth full and ravished.

'Yes, my love?'

'I'm not perfect,' she said with absolute seriousness.

'Yes, you are. For me, that is.'

And that was the way it continued to be.

CALL THE ONES YOU LOVE OVER THE HOLIDAYS!

Save $25 off future book purchases when you buy any four Harlequin® or Silhouette® books in October, November and December 2001,

PLUS

receive a phone card good for 15 minutes of long-distance calls to anyone you want in North America!

WHAT AN INCREDIBLE DEAL!

Just fill out this form and attach 4 proofs of purchase (cash register receipts) from October, November and December 2001 books, and Harlequin Books will send you a coupon booklet worth a total savings of $25 off future purchases of Harlequin® and Silhouette® books, AND a 15-minute phone card to call the ones you love, anywhere in North America.

Please send this form, along with your cash register receipts
as proofs of purchase, to:
In the USA: Harlequin Books, P.O. Box 9057, Buffalo, NY 14269-9057
In Canada: Harlequin Books, P.O. Box 622, Fort Erie, Ontario L2A 5X3
Cash register receipts must be dated no later than December 31, 2001.
Limit of 1 coupon booklet and phone card per household.
Please allow 4-6 weeks for delivery.

**I accept your offer! Enclosed are 4 proofs of purchase.
Please send me my coupon booklet
and a 15-minute phone card:**

Name: _____

Address: _____ City: _____

State/Prov.: _____ Zip/Postal Code: _____

Account Number (if available): _____

---

097 KJB DAGL
PHQ4013